Matthias' Leap of Faith

By: Maria C. De Aveiro Griffiths

Copywriter: 2024 by Maria C. De Aveiro Griffiths

eBook ISBN: 978-1-964451-54-1
Paperback ISBN: 978-1-964818-06-1
LCCN: 2024910463

All rights reserved. No part of this book may be reproduced, or transmitted in any form or by any means, electronic or mechanical, including photocopying, recording or by any information storage and retrieval system, without written permission from the publisher.

Table of Contents

Acknowledgements i

Chapter One 1

Chapter Two 3

Chapter Three 8

Chapter Four 11

Chapter Five 16

Chapter Six 20

Chapter Seven 24

Chapter Eight 28

Chapter Nine 31

Chapter Ten 33

Chapter Eleven 40

Chapter Twelve 43

Chapter Thirteen 46

Chapter Fourteen 51

Chapter Fifteen 54

Chapter Sixteen 57

Chapter Seventeen 59

Chapter Eighteen 62

Chapter Nineteen 64

Chapter Twenty 69

Chapter Twenty-One 75

Chapter Twenty-Two 77

Chapter Twenty-Three 82

Chapter Twenty-Four 84

Chapter Twenty-Five 88

Chapter Twenty-Six 91

Chapter Twenty-Seven 94

Chapter Twenty-Eight 97

Chapter Twenty-Nine 100

Chapter Thirty 103

Conclusion 106

References/sources: 107

About the Author 108

Acknowledgements

I would like to express a special thanks to David Griffiths, who played such a crucial role to bring this book to fruition. He has been a valued adviser and constructive critic. To him this book is lovingly dedicated.

I also like to acknowledge and thank the Penguin Bookwriters Publishing staff for their assistance to publish this book.

Chapter One

The bulk of Matthias day is often spent in the fields. After feeding the pigs, goats, and chickens and eating breakfast, he might spend the remainder of the day (with the exception of the noon-time meal) tending the crops. Chores take the form of plowing, hauling, sowing, cultivating, watering, harvesting—to name just a few. Winter offers no respite from mostly trimming fruit trees; it is the season to plant some grain crops so the rains may come and water them.

If Matthias is not busy in the fields, he might be found working on repairing outbuildings. Tasks include brushing the horses, donkey, greasing wagons, mending fences, repairing roofs, and making improvements to the house and barn. Besides contributing to the efficient functioning of the farm, a well-maintained barn and outbuildings are an important measure of Matthias's success and pride. He does hire seasonal laborers to assist on the farm.

Work is very difficult using donkeys and horses to do most of the labor in the fields. It requires many workers to trim the fruit trees in late winter, to fertilize and assist with harvest in late spring and early summer. Matthias hires many temporary workers to help keep things moving. Prior to harvest he tends the orchard and mostly monitors the workers on his own. Having four daughters and one son doesn't provide much labor needed to manage the vast daily work and chores required for the thirty acres of orchard. Mathias is a force to keep everything working like a symphony. It is his pride.

Early morning on a beautiful summer day is like any other day for Matthias. He and his donkey prepare to go out to work in his fruit orchard. He must inspect the fruit prior to harvest and see to it if water is necessary, for it has not rained in days. Today, the land reflects a yellow glow from the early morning bright sun. He pets the donkey and says, "It is going to be a hot one today." As if to expect an answer, he begins to harness the donkey like he does each morning, and begins to fill the huge wooden barrel secured to the back of the wooden trailer with fresh water. They are ready to go. They head off on their morning ritual. The donkey reluctantly starts off pulling the rugged trailer behind it. The fresh water weighs down the trailer as it has often done so on the extremely hot days.

Matthias and the donkey continue on the normal route around the edge of the orchard located along the upper hill of Alum Rock Park property line. The park starts at Mathias's property line and cascades down into a deep ravine to meet a river bed flowing between two mountains.

The park is neatly hidden with a canopy of trees that provide a refreshing cool getaway for folks to escape the summer heat. Alum Rock Park was founded in 1872 and is one of California's oldest municipal parks. Nestled within the Alum Rock Canyon in the foothills of the Diablo Range, the Park's 720 acres of natural, rugged beauty provide visitors with many leisure outdoor activities including hiking, horseback riding, bicycling, family and group picnicking, and of course just relaxing. Picnic tables, barbecue pits, water and restrooms are available in most picnic areas with lawns, and a children's playground in the mid-canyon area.

Chapter Two

1940s Alum Rock Park was a popular place to go to on a Saturday or Sunday after church. There was a trolley line running from downtown San Jose where families would pack their picnic baskets and go to spend the day.

The road leading to the park is narrow and descends down a spiraling road covered with tall overgrown trees. It creates a canopy with a cool breeze under the draping foliage that forms a tunnel all the way down to the river bed. The temperature in the park is about twenty degrees cooler which provides a welcome reprieve from the heat above. It used to be a best kept secret enjoyed mostly by the locals but word quickly spread and immigrants began to flock to the place to enjoy a weekend outing. Matthias's property line ends on top of the mountain overlooking the park.

The top of the mountain that leads to the park is camouflaged with shrubs and many trees that meet Mathias's property. It is also a perfect haven for animals to thrive. Matthias often hunts near his property line for turkeys, deer, quail and rabbit in his spare time.

After walking some distance with his donkey, he is startled and stops almost approaching the edge of his field. He hears a shuffling sound coming from the bushes just ahead. These bushes lead deep into the park. It is normal for him to carry a rifle on the wagon. He immediately reaches for his Winchester on the floorboard of the rugged old rusted trailer and charges after the sound. Moving in the direction of the sound, he leaves his donkey and trailer and feels the adrenaline rushing through his body. The pursuit intensifies as he remembers his previous successes hunting and capturing the wild animals. It provides a delightful addition to the diet of mostly chickens and pork to feed his family of seven. He feels lucky today and stays on the trail.

Matthias is now some distance into the park and begins to slow down. The thick shrubs under the canopy of tall trees make it difficult to penetrate the trail toward the place where he can hear the sound. He feels his shirt and pants tear on the wild blackberry bushes standing tall from the mother plant. Stubborn low branches dropping down from the trees and the thick brush on the ground slow him down but he fights to stay on the trail. Suddenly, he stops and freezes in his tracks. He notices a powerfully pungent, disgusting odor that makes his eyes water and looks around to locate the source of the smell. He figures the stench is coming from a decomposing dead animal. Matthias refocuses his attention to another shuffling sound in the bushes immediately ahead of him and decides to ignore the stench and keep going. There is a brief glimpse of what looks like the rump of a buck galloping a few yards ahead of him but it soon disappears. Wow! He thinks! A Buck! What a prize. Excited, he picks up the pace and stays on the trail.

The odor can no longer be ignored. It becomes more pungent and unbearable to the point that he pulls a handkerchief out of his back pocket and covers his mouth and nose to camouflage the odor. By now he is some distance away from his donkey but he continues to pursue the buck. After a while he is exhausted and pauses again to look for movement or noise but hears nothing. He decides to go a bit further in a very slow pace in the hope of surprising the animal. He approaches a small clearing and to his disappointment he has completely lost sight of the buck. The animal has completely vanished. Matthias stands and hangs his head in disappointment for losing the catch of his life.

The odor catches his attention again. It is overpowering as he stands in the clearing, so he moves to scout the woods for any sign of the decomposing animal carcass. He lifts his head up and looks straight ahead and freezes motionless. What his astonished eyes behold completely incapacitates him. Why, the stench is not of a decomposing animal. He is shocked at what he witnesses.

Matthias presses the handkerchief tighter over his mouth. Silently, he stares and finds courage to move slowly forward to identify the object and stumbles on a dead tree stump. He regains his composure and becomes mesmerized as his eyes are focused on a decomposing corpse hanging from a tall tree. He looks around for evidence or anything that might justify what he is witnessing. He immediately gets sick to his stomach and begins to throw up violently, perhaps from the stench and the grotesque naked body hanging lifeless before him. The decomposing body is of a woman. He studies the corpse but the stench is overwhelming as the summer heat has intensified the odor. The woman appears to be in her late twenties or early thirties. Her bloated decomposing skin indicates she has been dead for some time.

The exposure to the elements along with the hot summer temperature has taken a toll on the body. Her colorless face looks down to the ground and her eyes are closed and set deep into the eye sockets. She has long stringy black hair cascading down to her chest. She is naked with blotches of what appear to be bruises over her purple gray body. There is blood caked over her thighs and legs indicating foul play. It appears to be a rape and murder, not a suicide. It likely must have taken more than one person to elevate her to such a high position off the ground.

The thick tree branch that the rope is tied around is difficult to reach. The body hangs lifeless about five feet above the ground without anything under her feet which may have assisted her climb. It would require more than one person to perform such a gruesome deed, he thinks to himself. The strange thing Matthias notices is the area around the body is pristine and neat. There are no clothes or shoes anywhere near the scene of the crime and no foot impressions and his eyes don't detect any disturbances to the dry brown grass under her feet. How peculiar, he thinks to himself.

Matthias goes into shock with remorse and ponders what should he do. He decides to notify the local police some distance away down the mountain from his property but first he decides to relate the scene to his wife. He starts walking and realizes how weak his legs are and begins to stagger through the woods. Exhausted, he hits every branch and shrub as he fights his way through to reach back to the donkey. He climbs on the cart, throws his rifle against the wall of the trailer, and tries to get the donkey to move but the donkey is very content to rest from the heat and takes his time moving. The full water barrel and heat restrains the donkey from moving quickly. Matthias becomes impatient and hits the donkey but the animal meanders along the property line until it reaches home.

Matthias looks ragged in his clothes that have been shredded from fighting with the scrubs and tree limbs. He looks white as a ghost as he rushes into the house to share the news with his wife, Mary. She stares at the pitiful sight of her husband for a few seconds before he can start talking.

Mary says, "Oh my, you look awful! You look like you saw a ghost! What happened?"

He begins to rattle on as fast as his voice will allow him. She is confused as she listens intently to Matthias describing the scene. She becomes saddened as he relates the story but Matthias is talking so fast he doesn't leave room for her to ask him questions.

Finally, she interrupts and says, "Calm down!" He lowers his tone of voice and tries to relax but anxiety overtakes him and he starts speaking fast again. She can barely understand what he is trying to tell her. Mary rushes to the kitchen and gets Matthias a cup of water. He finally seems to calm down a bit and begins to tell her what he saw. She suggests he take the old stallion for a quicker ride to the police station. Mary remembers Mathias always goes out to the orchard and becomes surprised that he did not notice the smell before. Matthias looks at Mary and says, "Yes, Yes, that's what I will do".

He suddenly gets a burst of new energy and charges out the kitchen door down to the barn where the horse is put up. His little home is a one story cabin made of wood with white wash paint on the outside. It contains barely three small bedrooms, a small country kitchen, and a small living room. The four girls share one room. The boy is luckier he has one room to himself. Most of the homes surrounding their home have only one bedroom and house large families. There is no TV or radio at home but there is an old fashioned hand-winding record player that plays old records, a perfect evening treat for a gathering of family and friends.

Matthias approaches the stall and the tired old ragged looking horse is resting comfortably. Advanced in age and tired from working in the fields, it remains content to stay put. It is unimpressed with Matthias's urgency as he puts the bridle in its mouth and around its neck to drag it from the comfortable stall. The horse showing a sign of disapproval gives out a loud neigh but Matthias pats and rubs its head and side as a sign of reassurance. He manages to put on the saddle and climbs on but the horse decides not to move. He kicks the sides to get the horse going and still it refuses. Matthias loses his patience and gives it a couple of hard sharp kicks and the horse takes off in a blaze as Matthias hangs on to the reins for dear life. The horse speeds down the pathway and down the mountain leaving Matthias speechless at how much energy the old animal can display.

Chapter Three

They arrive at the local police station, a little one-story wooden frame building tucked against the foot hills in East Side San Jose that lead to the main entrance of Alum Rock Park. Matthias looks ragged and tired as he enters the building and approaches the officers on duty. He is somewhat reluctant because he does not speak English and does not know if the officers will understand his Portuguêse. Luckily, one officer happens to speak Portuguêse enough to understand Matthias. He starts to rapidly babble the scene of what he saw.

"Calm down! Relax!" the officers say.

Matthias looks nervous and beat up with dirt caked over his face. He begins relating the scene of the crime. Three suspicious officers stand nearby, silently sizing up Matthias's bruises, scratches from the thick shrubs. After the officers have made sense of what Matthias is saying, they get on their horses and ride up the mountain to the location of the scene. The officers and Matthias leave their horses on the edge of his property because of the dense foliage preventing the horses from entering.

Matthias leads them through the woods to the crime scene. The crime scene reveals itself as they approach. Before long the area is filled with police officers and an investigation is launched. For the moment Matthias is free to go home and continue his daily mundane tasks of running the orchard and farm. The police are puzzled with no leads to solve the case. As time goes by, Matthias is frequently called to the police station for questioning.

Mathias's Peach orchard

Matthias's inability to speak English leaves the local police a bit suspicious of the whole incident. But, all efforts to solve the case with no suspects go cold. The murder is headline news throughout the community and people demand answers. The police do confirm the woman was raped and murdered just as Mathias reported. This puts tremendous pressure on the local police department to solve the case. The park is a hideaway for many families from the summer heat and the murder creates an unsettling unease among the community that venture into the park. Continuous pressure is put on the police department to solve the crime.

More agents are called from different parts of California to work on the case. First thing, the investigators try to identify the woman but without a report of a missing person she is never identified. Days, weeks, months, and years go by but the murderers are never found. With the lack of evidence to solve the case the police begin to look at Matthias as a prime suspect.

Chapter Four

Madeira is a province of Portugal nestled in the eastern Atlantic. This group of islands lies some three hundred and sixty miles from the African coast, at roughly the same latitude as Casablanca. Funchal is the Capital of Madeira. Madeira has an area of three hundred and eight square miles. It is bounded for the most part by high and forbidding volcanic cliffs that fall almost vertically into the sea.

The beginning of settlement on Madeira dates to 1425. Considerable progress must have already been made by the time Henry the Navigator confirmed ownership of the land by the discoverers of Madeira on behalf of King Joao I. By 1450 Funchal and Machico soon developed into flourishing towns, the former becoming the major trading center in the Atlantic.

The great Christopher Columbus lived on the island for several years after marrying Dona Filipa, the daughter of Bartolomeo Perestrelo. He received navigational documents from his father-in-law and other Portuguêse seafarers from which he obtained important information for the discovery of the New World.

Columbus fathered his only son and lived between Madeira and Port Santo for several years. He was convinced by the exotic plant remains washed up on Madeira's shores that sailing westward would bring him to the spice island of the Indies. He left to sail to Lisbon, the Capital of Portugal, located five hundred miles away to the East to raise funds for an expedition to test his theory.

Madeira Island is the main port for ships to resupply as they venture to discover unknown lands. Many sailors and navigators are well familiar with the island which provides a bounty of fresh fruits, water and supplies for their crew. Machico City dips down the mountain side to sea level, making it convenient to disembark and load vessels. It was the port of entry for early settlers who arrived in Machico to settle the Island. It is a thriving community now.

It is January 20, 1873 in this village called Santo da Serra some fifteen kilometers from Funchal and six kilometers from Machico where Matthias, the youngest of three boys is born to a destitute and poor family who survives off the land they own and cultivate for food. Like most islanders the family struggles to provide for their families. Employment is difficult especially in the rugged high mountain villages and wages are the lowest in Europe. Meats and crops are bartered among the neighboring residents to provide extra protein and vegetables for the family. Rice, pasta, spices, sugar, and salt are luxuries and well-cherished. The lack of money makes bartering the only way to do business among the villagers.

Homes are sparsely located around the mountains. The dwelling Matthias lives in with his family consists of two buildings; one for a kitchen and a separate building for sleeping. The roofs are made of thatch from the fall wheat harvest. The beds are stuffed with straw and refreshed with each fall harvest. The kitchen is used for cooking, eating, and socializing around the fire especially in the winter in and the cold nights. The family encircles the fire while grandmother prepares a nice evening tea made of garden herbs such as mint, fennel, or rosemary. The family shares the activities of the day until the ambers become covered with ashes, giving the signal that it is bedtime.

Matthias as a young lad is a quick learner with strong common sense. He does miniscule tasks to assist with farming. One of his favorite pastimes is to follow the free range chickens to their hidden nest to steal eggs for grandmother's cooking.

He remembers his grandmother saying, "Leave one egg so the hen will continue to lay."

At age eleven he is ready to start working daily with his two older brothers, two uncles, father and grandfather. The ladies stay home and do house chores and feed the animals. He learns quickly and adapts to the daily routine of farming. The rugged steep terrain on the mountainside demands tier farming. Hoes, shovels, sickles, picks, and hand tools are used to cultivate the land. The land is broken into small parcels and leveled with stone walls. The parcels are small but easy to cultivate and crops can be planted on the fertile soil the year round.

It is a daunting and challenging task to feed a family of ten individuals through the year and it requires everyone in the family to contribute. The land is an inheritance passed down from Matthias's great grandparents to his grandmother. The land provides enough food for the family and extra for bartering. The villagers look out for each other to make sure everyone survives the cold harsh winters.

His home is located high on the mountains in a very remote region about seven kilometers from the closest city of Machico located down at the sea shore. The distance prevents him from attending school and socializing with boys his age. On his free time Matthias often wanders through the eucalyptus forest on the top the mountain above his home. Here he lies on the crackling dry eucalyptus leaves and passes hours contemplating and dreaming about his future. His mind drifts toward elaborate and wild possibilities and he wants them to become a reality.

On his way home he picks up falling wood sticks and small branches of dead wood. Back home grandmother uses them for cooking and keeping the kitchen warm during the cold nights. Grandma is always thrilled to see him with a load of wood that she doesn't even notice how long he's been gone.

Matthias at age sixteen has already mastered the farming skills and becomes bored. He becomes an asset to the family as he can manage the crops all year round. He is a fast learner so now he can plant and harvest and care for the livestock. The livestock is limited to two pigs, several chickens, and a cow that provides milk, cheese and butter, and eventually meat for the family. Chickens are the main source of meat for the family most months of the year. A pig is butchered at Christmas time when the community partakes in dressing the pig and sharing the meat with a big celebration.

At age eighteen Matthias already stands six feet tall and towers over his two brothers. He has a slender body, inset baby blue eyes with thick bushy eyebrows and dark thick black hair. The dominant high cheek bones highlight his long oblong thin face as he displays a wide bright smile that lights up a room. He is a ladies' man. He is grandmother's favorite shining star. He is a handsome young man who stands out among his family members. He is the family entertainer who likes to tell jokes and dance after dinner when the family huddles around the open fire pit. The pit is located in the corner of the kitchen room. Matthias loves the attention he gets when he is in the spotlight, not to mention the attention he gets from the local young ladies when he encounters them.

Now at age nineteen he has become restless with the daily chores and a routine that seems to go nowhere. He wants more for his life. As he lies down on the small patch of grass overlooking the valley below, he glances into the distance and his eyes catch a glimpse of a cruise ship sailing some distance away. His mind begins to wander and he starts to dream of being on a ship sailing away to a life somewhere else where he can work and achieve something better for himself. He often shares his dream with his family especially his brothers, but his family thinks he is just a dreamer. Unlike him, his brothers are comfortable in the life they lead.

Madeira Island offers little in the way of economic or educational opportunity. Even though surrounded by such deep waters, the people of Madeira have turned their backs to the sea. The island's tiny fishing fleets employ only a handful of hardy adventurers who fish in the sea around the island. Instead most Madeirans make their living from hard terrace farming. They tend the narrow strips of land using shovels, picks, and sometimes cows to till the soil because there is no space on the terraces for machinery. Sugar, known as "white gold", made some of the early settlers rich until competition from New Worlds plantations drove the price down. The lack of jobs and money makes Mathias more restless than ever. Hard work in the fields, a strong family work ethic, strong morals along with a strong Catholic background are what molded Matthias from the start.

In 1895 The Island's economy is bursting by the large number of European tourists visiting for the winter, or staying in Madeira en route to postings in South America and the Far East. The port of Funchal, now the Capital of Madeira, is bursting with the activity of people coming and going to the Island. Matthias hears of the activities from neighbors who visit the city and share the information. He is desperate to visit Funchal to check things out.

Chapter Five

On a beautiful spring day Matthias decides to take a walk to Funchal instead of the eucalyptus forest. Funchal is fifteen kilometers away. He will leave early in the morning and take the shortest route down the sides of the levadas. The levadas (from the Portuguêse verb "levar" – to carry) are a system of channels or aqueducts running many kilometers, mostly bordering mountains but also going through them. Several of these waterways stretch over rugged rocks, to bring water from different sources to its intermediate or final uses. The water canals were built by slaves and contract workers who worked for the early settlers. These secluded paths are well known to the villagers as walking routes. Matthias walks along the levadas to speed his walk to Funchal. After a long walk he approaches the mountains overlooking the city.

Funchal is an elegant city, once dubbed "little Lisbon" by visiting mariners because of the grandeur of its cathedral and harbor-side buildings. The city resembles a huge amphitheater, sheltered by a semicircle of hills with open views across the harbor out to the sea.

It is a foggy day and Mathias cannot see clearly to the harbor below. The fog rolls over the mountains and camouflages the city. A trip to Funchal is seldom taken because of the long distance from home. It's a trip the family takes once a year to purchase clothing or household necessities. As the fog lifts with the mid-morning sun, he looks down to the harbor and between patches of fog he notices an unknown shape docked at the harbor. His eyes attempt to penetrate the morning mist and the fog but he cannot determine what the shape is until he comes farther down the mountain. As he descends the mountain he fetches a ride in a sliding wicker basket mounted on wooden runners, so that it becomes possible to cover the two kilometer descent from Monte to Livramento in ten minutes. The toboggan is a great way to speed down the cobblestone streets. This has been the mode of transportation down the steep mountains for years. As the fog lifts he can see the shape of the object clearly.

"Why it is a Clipper ship," he says.

He is intrigued. Admiring it as he is still some distance away, he continues to remain focused on the ship so much so that he runs into a couple of people going the opposite direction. Matthias has never seen a Chipper ship and the excitement overtakes him and he begins to run toward the harbor.

As Matthias admires the majestic ship he comes upon a group of five young men around his age huddled together, talking softly as if a secret is being shared. He walks closer and manages to overhear them talking about the news circulating among the people that the ship docked at the harbor is recruiting workers who want to sail to Hawaii with a promise of work and housing. The men who are all single are puzzled because they have no idea what Hawaii is or where it is located but this doesn't seem to affect their excitement and the thought of a new adventure.

Wow! Matthias thinks. Is this for real? He listens intently as the young men plan their opportunity to escape from Madeira Island on a voyage to an unknown world named Hawaii. The thought draws Matthias's attention.

"A new adventure," the five young men say to each other. "Oh, yeah!" they all agree. "That means leaving the Island and our families," one announces. Another says, "Yeah!" They all agree. They all pause a minute in thought.

Matthias is intrigued and chimes in, "I am interested in joining your group. I want to be part of this too!"

The young men look at Matthias. They look at each other, pause a second before they agree to welcome him. They all have the same dream of reaching a better life. Matthias has been dreaming of a new life and here is the ultimate opportunity for him. He encourages himself to take it.

The young men shout, "Hooray, let's do it!"

They make a solemn agreement to stay together and help one another through the journey no matter what happens. Matthias feels exhilarated at the thought of being accepted into the group for an adventure of a lifetime. The promise of a job and a better life is captivating. He is beside himself with joy as he says to himself, "What an adventure. Wow!"

The Clipper ship plans to stay docked for a few more days to restock before setting sail. The young men agree to meet in two days to go and see the ship's recruiter. The men all scatter toward their homes to inform their families of their decision. Matthias is ecstatic and eager as he walks away to share the news with his family. He picks up speed and starts running back up and disappears behind the mountains along the lavadas. It will take the rest of the day to get home.

He arrives home exhausted and out of breath. His mother asks, "Where have you been?"

Thinking he was in the forest foraging for wood all day, his grandma says, "Where is the wood?"

"No," he responds, "I went to Funchal."

"Why?" says grandmother "You've been gone all day."

Chapter Six

Matthias has a sparkle in his eyes as he shares the story with his family and his two elder brothers - Louis and Norberto. He urges his brothers to join him, fully expecting that they will. However, his brothers have a strong sense of loyalty to the family and decline his offer. As the family is aging, the boys feel a deep connection to their kin and refuse to leave. The rest of his family - three cousins, two uncles, his grandparents, and parents - consider his decision crazy, believing that he is venturing into an unknown world full of empty promises.

His mother finds the idea terrifying and exclaims, "Embarking on a journey halfway across the globe to an unknown world? You truly are crazy!" The whole family echoes her sentiment, loudly exclaiming, "You're insane!" She repeats herself, stating, "Embarking on a journey halfway across the globe to an unknown world? You must be out of your mind, Matthias!" Grandfather interjects, "A trip from Europe to Hawaii can take months to complete." His father interrupts, insisting, "You're completely mad to even consider such a perilous journey." His grandmother adds, "You should stay here with your family, where you belong." "Besides," his uncle chimes in, "you won't know a soul when you arrive, if you arrive at all." Matthias listens silently to his family's concerns and advice, refraining from responding. His two brothers sit on a wooden bench, gazing silently at the dirt floor of the kitchen, captivated by the warmth of the crackling fire. Matthias' family is overwhelmed by the news, urging him to stay home and abandon his wild dreams. Everyone is shocked, and a heavy silence hangs in the air as they listen to Matthias passionately make his case. Eventually, the family realizes that Matthias is determined and resolute in his decision to leave. They settle down and manage to enjoy the meal that his mother and grandmother had spent the entire day preparing. A hearty soup made of collard greens, sausage, potatoes, pasta, and pork is served, accompanied by freshly baked bread made by grandmother earlier in the afternoon. After all the discussion, Matthias is determined to take the risk regardless. In the early evening, he rushes around to find an old, ragged small suitcase that belonged to his grandparents some years earlier. He locates it tucked away under the bed in a corner against the wall. He reaches for it, wipes off the dust, and begins to pack the bare necessities he will need. Although he goes to bed, sleep eludes him throughout the night. The excitement keeps him awake, pondering about his future. A sweat overtakes his body as he realizes how nervous he is about taking this leap of faith.

Morning arrives, and he walks out of the sleeping chambers, a separate building used solely for sleeping, located a few yards down the hill from the kitchen building. He retrieves his suitcase and walks up the hill to the kitchen. He is astonished to see his family lined up in front of the kitchen door, waiting for him. He notices the expressions of terror and disappointment on their faces, especially his mother's. The scene briefly creates doubt as he contemplates his decision. He remembers the warmth his family provided him over the years, but his urge to leave is stronger.

Matthias is a jolly fellow, and his smile illuminates his face as he looks at each family member and embraces them with a kiss. His father asks, "Aren't you going to eat before you leave?" "No," Matthias replies. "I have a long trip and must get going." His father and mother are the most difficult to bid farewell to. His mother breaks down sobbing, and his father's eyes well up with tears when their gazes meet. He looks directly at his son, walks up to him, and hands him a few escudos (money). He says, "It's not much, but you will need it," then walks away with tears streaming down his cheeks without saying goodbye. Matthias feels helpless and hurt but understands his father's reaction. Matthias is his father's youngest and most beloved son, and seeing his father abruptly leave without saying goodbye is incredibly difficult for him. There is so much Matthias wants to say to his father, but the opportunity slips away as his father walks off. Luis and Norberto are so angry and upset with Matthias' decision to leave that they disappear into the fields in protest and do not want to see Matthias to bid him farewell.

He begins walking away as his family continues to stand, looking horrified and hoping he will change his mind and turn around to come home. The family is awestruck that Matthias is so determined and serious about leaving. Instead, he disappears into the mountainside. Once out of sight, he leaps with excitement, feeling an overwhelming sense of freedom. He starts running towards his destination in Funchal. Matthias arrives exhausted yet energetic as he joins up with the five young men whom he had met two days prior. They exchange their names for the first time: Matthias, Michael, Dennis, Frank and Miguel. The young men begin to walk, getting in line to talk with the recruiter. Michael stops and shouts, "Wait! Are you sure this is what you want to do?" All six men glance at each other, pause for a few seconds, and unanimously say, "Yes! Let's go!"

It is April 1895 when Matthias embarks on an unknown journey in pursuit of a better life. He feels both excited and nervous about his new adventure. The ship is coming from Lisbon, Portugal, and the Clipper ship stops in Madeira to resupply and recruit workers on its routine voyage from Europe to the Hawaiian Islands. This ship, carrying 450 human souls, will fill a large void with workers who will cultivate the vast sugar-cane and pineapple fields of the Hawaiian Islands. Many Madeirans and Western European men struggle with the lack of job opportunities in their own countries, and they take the risk of leaving everything behind for a chance at success, including Matthias. They abandon property, community life, and families to take a leap of faith for this opportunity. Matthias, especially concerned about leaving his family behind, including his mom and dad and the familiar homestead, briefly doubts his decision and wonders, "Am I making a big mistake?"

In the years from 1878 to 1913, the transportation of emigrants began with a German sailing ship called the Priscilla, which took a group of 123 single men and families from Madeira to Hawaii. The journey took 120 days. Over the next thirty-five years, 28 ships, both sailing and steam, transported over 25,000 Portuguese people to Hawaii. The sailing ships took between 92 and 156 days, while the steamships completed the journey in 53 to 76 days.

An early picture of a clipper ship

Chapter Seven

They proceed to walk to the dock, joining a long line of people who share the same dream. Matthias notices men, women, and children all lined up, ready to give up everything in pursuit of a better life. He looks at the panoramic view of the mountains cradling the city of Funchal, which resembles a Christmas tree adorned with white stucco homes, red tile roofs, large windows, and tropical plants and flowers. He continues to admire the city as he waits. The homes are embedded on the mountainside, reaching up to the sky. The mosaic cobblestone streets, with their white and gray tiles, give way to flower gardens, especially the hydrangeas that cling to the winding street corners and home gardens. Matthias is captivated by its beauty, and tears fill his eyes at the sight of leaving.

Frank nudges him on the shoulder to continue as the line moves slowly forward, each person waiting patiently until they reach the recruiters. In the distance, they can see four tables set up to process the large number of people. A careful screening, along with lots of questions, delays the line's progress. The recruiters look intimidating as the men approach. They are strong, big men dressed in heavy linen shirts and black vests. They look unshaven and speak with strong, loud, hoarse voices. "Skills and trade knowledge are what the recruiters are looking for," shouts a man in line. "People must have a skill or trade in order to be accepted on the voyage," he continues. The young men become a little uneasy and wonder if they have the right skills and trade knowledge that the recruiters are seeking. As Matthias stands in line, waiting his turn, his mind drifts back to the warmth of his humble family home. The home consists of a small kitchen building and a triangular-shaped building for the bedrooms. The doors are always open to family and neighbors, who visit to share meals or a glass of wine. Family and neighbors seek each other out to share stories, creating a true sense of openness to anyone who visits. Most gatherings take place in the kitchen or outside, where everyone can come together. Community news and gossip are shared, fostering close bonds. For a brief moment, Matthias' eyes fill with tears as he takes one last look at Funchal, the beautiful city he is leaving behind.

The line begins to move again, and Matthias refocuses his attention on a family of four huddled together as they inch forward. Matthias observes that the family is being turned away, though he does not know the reason. He is saddened as he listens to them plead their case to no avail. The four recruiters respond forcefully and with certainty, sealing the fate of the family. Matthias' heart breaks as he witnesses the disappointment in their eyes, knowing they are walking away in tears. He also notices men and women with young children clinging to their mothers, patiently waiting their turn to reach the front of the line and learn their own fate.

Like Matthias, many of the people in line carry small handbags containing all their belongings, while some have only the clothes on their backs. The air is heavy with sadness as the people remain silent, gazing at their beloved home island, unsure if they will ever see their families again. The leap of faith they have taken casts a shadow of uncertainty on their faces.

Finally, it is their turn. The six men stay together as they approach a table. Each of them is asked a series of questions: What is your occupation? What skills do you possess? Do you have a family? Why do you wish to leave? Each man answers the questions and is given paperwork to complete. Among the six young men, only Frank and Jose can read and write. The two help the others fill out their paperwork, offering themselves to the care of the recruiters. Once the recruiter reviews the completed forms, they are informed that they have been accepted. The six men are directed to join others in line to board a rowboat that will transport them to the ship. Overwhelmed with excitement, they chat amongst themselves, all agreeing that their age and lack of family likely played a role in their selection. As they board the crowded rowboat, they wonder if it will withstand the weight. The anticipation of a new life is contagious and thrilling, lifting the spirits of the voyagers. As the rowboat nears the ship, everyone is captivated by its massive size that looms over the rowboat as they approach. Matthias and his fellow immigrants board the Clipper ship, marveling at the towering masts that rise over a hundred feet in height. The passengers are awestruck by the ship's magnitude and strength, instilling a sense of security within them. They willingly embark on the Clipper, placing their trust in the ship's Captain to guide them to their destination. Once all the immigrants from the Madeira Islands are on board, they are instructed to gather with the others already on board from Europe. Captain Blitz introduces himself and addresses the passengers on the sturdy wooden foredeck. With all 450 anxious souls listening attentively, he begins to speak. "Welcome aboard!" Captain Blitz says, speaking slowly as an interpreter translates his words into Portuguese. "We are headed for the Hawaiian Islands, a collection of islands situated in the Pacific Ocean," he explains. The people exchange puzzled glances, as the majority of them have not heard of the Hawaiian Islands.

The Hawaiian Planters' Society commenced recruiting Portuguese contract workers, initially in 1878 from the Madeira Islands and later, in 1880, from the Azores. Starting in 1878, several ships transported over 3,300 Portuguese men from these islands to Hawaii. Many of the men brought their wives, children, and other relatives along with them. Over the course of these years, immigration brought nearly 16,000 Portuguese individuals to the Hawaiian Islands, concluding in 1911.

The native Hawaiians referred to the Portuguese immigrants who arrived on their island as "Pokiki." These newcomers were devout followers of the Roman Catholic faith, known for their strong family bonds. Most of them were of short stature, slender build, and had dark tans acquired from toiling in the fields under the sun. Since only a minority of these immigrants could read or write, they relied heavily on oral traditions, resulting in the preservation of the cultural practices they brought with them. One such tradition embraced by the Hawaiian natives was the Portuguese ukulele, which became an integral part of their music culture and gained widespread fame.

Chapter Eight

The clipper ship Matthias finds himself aboard is capable of sailing at a speed of fifteen to eighteen nautical miles per hour. Its top speed has been measured at twenty knots. The clipper's dimensions are: 325 feet long, 53 feet beam, and 30 feet depth of hold. It has four complete decks and four masts, three of which are square-rigged. The ship spreads 16,000 square feet of canvas in a single suit of sails. It is constructed with 2,380 tons of white oak in its frame, 1,500,000 feet of hard pine in the keelson, planking, etc., 300 tons of iron, and 50 tons of copper. The passengers are speechless at the ship's enormous size.

The clipper is relatively narrow for its length. Unfortunately, the people on board are cramped and each is seeking a place to sleep for the night. The lower levels are crowded and contain a large empty hold where the immigrants will stay during the trip. The limited space on the upper deck forces many men, including Matthias and his five new friends, to find a more spacious place—though in rough weather, they may be showered with spray from high waves. There are other accommodations, such as separate berths for the crew and suites for wealthier passengers. The two lower decks are used for storage and kitchens with food preparation areas. Eventually, everyone settles down and adjusts to the confined living conditions onboard.

Captain Blitz, a burly character named Joseph P. Blitz, appears intimidating at first glance—a rough-looking man indeed. His skin is dark brown from exposure to the sun and wind. He has an unkempt, dark brown beard that reaches his chest and a mustache above his lip. His hair is as stiff as bristles on a hairbrush. He is tall, almost as tall as Matthias, and has a scar over his left eye from a previous altercation with a shipmate. He wears the scar with pride, as it represents his triumph in a disagreement. It serves as a warning to others who dare challenge him. Captain Blitz cuts an unusual figure in his seafaring attire, with a white ruffled shirt, black pants that reach just above his knee-high leather boots, and a wide black belt around his waist. A cutlass is strapped to his left side, and he wears a black oilskin hat that partly obscures his thick eyebrows. Standing confidently on the captain's deck, he commands the attention and obedience of his motley crew of twenty-nine men. The passengers, in turn, study him carefully as he scans over them and the crew.

Shortly after receiving a brief instruction from the captain, Matthias' voyage begins with Captain Blitz's command to unfurl the sails. "Ready to sail," he shouts. Still at the wharf, the jib, fore topsail, and main topmast staysail are released; the bowline is cast off, the mizzen topsail is set free, and the stern-fast is released. The clipper emerges into the breeze and gracefully makes its way from the shore, heading directly toward the vast sea.

At the command, the passengers begin to celebrate their departure, while those on the shore bid them farewell with waves and cheers. The ship is heavily laden, both with cargo and passengers. It carries a variety of cargo, including Madeira wine, water, food, and essential supplies for the passengers, as well as merchandise for the merchants awaiting their arrival in Hawaii. On board, Matthias notices men and families speaking different European languages and is informed that they hail from various European countries. He and his friends feel lost and unable to communicate with these passengers. However, Captain Blitz is able to speak English.

The clipper sets off on its journey, leaving the port of Madeira. The passengers gather on the ship's deck, watching their beloved island fade into the horizon. It is likely that Captain Blitz discussed the length of the voyage, the name of the ship, and the planned route, which involves sailing south on the Atlantic Ocean, rounding the perilous Cape Horn, and then heading north to the Pacific Ocean. The journey to Hawaii covers a distance of 13,045 miles. Depending on the weather and other factors, it may take several months for Captain Blitz's Clipper to reach the port in Honolulu, Hawaii. But for now, the passengers are too excited and overwhelmed to fully grasp Captain Blitz's announcements, even as the ship glides gently through the ocean with a soft breeze. The crew, engaged in raising the anchor and unfurling the sails, are dressed casually in dirty white shirts and brown pants that hang below their knees. Most of them go about their duties barefoot. Many have missing front teeth from scurvy and cover their heads with faded rags to secure their long hair. Having spent their lives on the ship, the crew performs their duties mechanically, always ready at a moment's notice. They concentrate on their work, oblivious to the passengers who stand around celebrating or watching in awe as the crew works in perfect harmony.

Meanwhile, the passengers stake out space on the ship. Soon enough, the seawater becomes rough, causing the ship to sway from side to side and resulting in seasickness. For days, the passengers contend with vomiting and dry heaves, as the constant motion and inability to keep food down make many of them ill. Numerous buckets are placed around the main passengers' hold, serving as necessities for both toilets and sea sickness, as well as others for drinking water. Each morning, a crewmember, usually someone guilty of neglect or irritating the captain, carries the full buckets to the upper deck and empties them overboard into the sea.

Chapter Nine

Clipper ships were primarily constructed in British and American shipyards, although France, Brazil, the Netherlands, and a few other nations also produced some. They were built mainly between 1830 and 1870 and sailed across the world, particularly on the trade routes between the United Kingdom and its colonies in the East. These trade routes included trans-Atlantic voyages to and from Hawaii in the Pacific, as well as journeys from New York to San Francisco and back, around Cape Horn, and the well-established tea routes from China.

Cape Horn can be found at the tip of South America, in a latitude known as the Furious Fifties. In this latitude, there are no land masses below Cape Horn along the entire circumference of the Earth. Winds blow freely and steadily at these latitudes, with an average speed of eleven miles per hour in the month of April. The temperature during the day averages fifty degrees Fahrenheit, and at night, the average temperature is thirty-five degrees Fahrenheit, which is three degrees above freezing. It is currently a chilly autumn in the Southern Latitudes.

After a pleasant journey across the equator towards the tip of South America, the weather gradually becomes colder. The passengers are unprepared for the colder weather, and many huddle together to keep warm. There is a noticeable chill in the air at Cape Horn, which marks the northern boundary of the Drake Passage where the Atlantic and Pacific Oceans meet. The waters around Cape Horn are particularly dangerous due to strong winds, large waves, strong currents, and icebergs. These hazards have given Cape Horn a notorious reputation as a graveyard for sailors. The Drake Passage is a narrow path through the hundreds of islands that comprise the tip of South America. It stretches for one hundred and fifty miles and at its narrowest point, it may be only half a mile wide. In the sheltered waters of the narrow Drake Passage, Captain Blitz feels confident in this voyage, given his previous successful trips. He sees this journey as another achievement to be proud of and something he can boast about to his shipmates. To him, navigating the treacherous "Horn" seems like a breeze. He knows that the rough currents around Cape Horn are temporary and looks forward to encountering a vast, calmer sea.

As the voyage continues, everyone gets along despite the crowded conditions on the ship. Both passengers and crew share a common goal of reaching their destination as quickly as possible. Spirits are high among the passengers, and they find reasons to celebrate with the wine they brought, accompanied by singing and dancing to help pass the time. Some men gather on deck to play cards and games.

Chapter Ten

It could be said that Captain Blitz's luck had run out during this voyage. The wind around the equator, which the Clipper needed to cross in order to reach Hawaii, came to a standstill. This windless band around the equator, known as the Doldrums, often left ships becalmed. The Clipper's sails hung lifeless in the still air, with no wind to move them. Days and weeks passed by, and the usually swift Clipper ship remained adrift in the calm ocean. People were no longer celebrating; they were bored and discouraged. Restlessness grew, and tempers flared.

Captain Blitz recruited Matthias and his five friends, whom he had gotten to know well: Matthias, Michael, Miguel, Frank, Dennis, and Jose. He also recruited seven other young men to help maintain order on the ship. Food and water supplies were nearly depleted, and the crew began rationing them until they eventually ran out.

Conditions on the ship became dismal. Men resorted to collecting seawater in pails and boiling it desperately for a drink. The lack of food and water caused illness, especially among young children. Most people sat spread out throughout the upper deck, seeking shade from the sails in the scorching heat. Fights broke out among frustrated passengers, demanding more food and water and grabbing whatever they could in their desperation. Captain Blitz tried to maintain order by threatening to throw the defiant ones overboard, which calmed things down momentarily.

Weeks turned into months without sighting any land. Many believed they would die at sea. Passengers huddled together, praying for wind and rain so they could collect fresh water to drink. Captain Blitz delivered several speeches to encourage the passengers and maintain order, but desperation grew. Men attempted to fish by dropping makeshift nets overboard, but more often than not, they retrieved the nets empty. Panic ensued as days passed in the vastness of the equatorial Pacific Ocean, with only meager catches of fish and no fresh water to drink. Some men drank the ocean's saltwater and became delirious, and their behavior became very difficult to control. The crew and the selected men took charge, breaking up frequent fights among the angry and desperate crowd. The situation on the Clipper appeared grim. There are rumors among the passengers that their fellow travelers are dying. Often at night, Matthias and his friends hear the crew dumping something overboard in the darkness. Hearing this, Matthias and his friends become suspicious that the rumors may be true. They begin to keep track of the sickly individuals, waiting to see them disappear. One in particular is a young boy who frequently wanders lost around the upper deck. Somehow, he boarded the ship without any family. The boy, along with two other men, also disappears without notice from the passengers. Matthias and his friends dare not ask the crew or the captain for fear of inciting panic among the passengers.

The stagnant air in the main passenger hold compels people to come up to the upper deck for fresh air regularly. The overpowering stench of vomit and waste continues. Passengers start spending most of their time on deck, especially in the early morning and late evening, despite the scorching equatorial sun, because at least there is fresh air there.

After months of being stranded at sea, hopelessness engulfs the ship. Everyone acknowledges the grim reality that they are doomed to die from starvation and thirst. Passengers grow intolerant of one another, becoming easily angered over the smallest things. Then, early one morning, a scout from the lookout shouts, "LAND, LAND! Straight ahead!" The ship's crew and passengers are alerted by the scout's ecstatic cries. The news fills everyone with awe and excitement. Though the equatorial sun beats down relentlessly, a gentle breeze carries the clipper forward as the crew hastily raises the sails. Captain Blitz reaches for his spyglass.

The ship comes alive, and the passengers are infused with newfound energy. Everyone crams onto the upper deck, standing shoulder to shoulder, eagerly anticipating the sight of land. However, it remains a distant image on the hazy horizon. Men gather by the side of the ship, attempting to narrow their focus to the direction pointed out by the lookout, but they see nothing. "WHERE? WHERE?" some passengers yell. Silence descends over the ship as they anxiously await a glimpse of the long-awaited land. Then, cheers break out as a silhouette of land starts to emerge on the distant horizon, astonishing their eyes. Some passengers rub their eyes, trying to confirm what they see. The ship erupts in jubilant cheers, and celebrations ensue with swirling dances and applause. "Hawaii!" some yell. "Hooray!" others cry. "We are approaching our new home. We made it!" Hooray! Hooray! The crew is caught up in the celebration. But as Captain Blitz looks through his spyglass, he is shocked by what he sees! The landmass appears to be something other than Hawaii. Even the crew is deceived into believing they are approaching the harbor of Honolulu, Hawaii.

In the meantime, a frenzy overtakes the ship. The ladies run around trying to fix their soiled clothes, which look like rags from months at sea. They try to fix their untidy hair and freshen up their appearance after months of neglect. Their thin, pale faces are not as attractive, but their spirits are high at the thought of finally reaching their destination. They gain enough energy and enthusiasm to busy themselves securing their scattered belongings. The men are still mesmerized by what they see. They can't take their eyes off the huge landmass as the ship approaches the shore.

The excitement among the passengers turns into a chorus of singing. It is a symphony of music with different instruments playing together to create a delightful melody. It is hard to believe that just a few hours earlier, these same people were barely alive, and now they are filled with energy, hope, and joy. Matthias is captivated by all the excitement. "What a sight!" he says to himself with a big grin. There are women, children, and a few men who are too weak to participate in the celebration, but they are encouraged and manage a smile of approval. They gain more energy when fellow passengers help prepare them to disembark from the ship.

The ship arrives near the spacious dock where two other clippers are taking on supplies. The word "Hawaii" is not heard. Instead, the passengers hear the crew and Captain Blitz talking amongst themselves, mentioning "San Francisco." "San Francisco!" a passenger overhears and shouts. "Where is San Francisco?" another asks. It turns out that the Clipper has drifted so far off course that the current has brought the ship into the harbor of San Francisco, California, instead of Honolulu, Hawaii. The Clipper has drifted 2,400 miles off course and is now on the western edge of the United States. Captain Blitz is speechless and confirms this to the waiting passengers, who become confused about what to do. Although bewildered, they are eager to disembark. The passengers begin murmuring to one another: what should we do, they inquire? Uncertain of their destiny, they all gather closely together on the dock and await further instructions. Captain Blitz affirms once again that they are indeed in San Francisco, California, and requests a government representative along with two interpreters. There is a considerable amount of murmuring among the passengers, who are unsure of their fate. Captain Blitz gives control of the crowd to the representative. He attempts to calm the frightened passengers as they apprehend their unknown future. He says, "Please listen to me and hear what I have to say." He repeats it a few times until silence falls upon the somber crowd. "You can all remain here in San Francisco harbor and take a week's rest while the ship is restocked. You will be taken care of, and after a week, you will reboard the ship and continue your journey to Hawaii. In the meantime, accommodations will be provided for you in a hotel or boarding house, and your food and supply needs will be met. We will all reconvene here to board the ship on this day next week."

The crowd erupts, shouting and screaming in protest. Go back on the ship? No way! They exclaim. The passengers are terrified at the idea of returning to the ship, where they nearly lost their lives. The representative realizes he cannot ease their anxiety after the horrifying experience they just went through. He begs them to calm down. He goes on, "If you want to stay here, we have plenty of job opportunities in the San Francisco Bay area." The entire group of passengers falls silent and listens attentively, then bursts into cheers and applause with great enthusiasm at the news.

Matthias and his friends are overwhelmed with emotion at the news. He notices a bustling seaside with lots of activity. People are going to and fro, and the harbor is well-settled with rows of buildings that extend to endless streets. There are many stores and horse-drawn wagons carrying cargo, supplies, and people. Matthias and his friends are pleased with what they see and are eager to stay.

The representative continues, "If you decide to stay, you will work for the government, and work is this: based on your trade knowledge, the government will provide you with a boarding house for you to live in and food for six months to allow you time to establish your own household," he continues. "You will be paid fifty-five cents per day. You will work from sun up to sundown, and no other benefits will be provided other than what I have mentioned." After such a difficult voyage, passengers are satisfied with what they hear and immediately agree to sign on to work. To them, it is a relief not to have to go back to sea. The passengers agree to stay in San Francisco and make the best of their misfortune. The emigrants have one week to rest and regain their strength. They are to report back to the dock for further instructions. Once again, a line begins to form for the passengers to be assigned accommodations. Every effort is made to keep families together. Matthias and his friends are all assigned to the same boarding house.

The San Francisco seashore is a bustling place with many people wandering the streets, going about their business. For the first time, the men see Chinese individuals mingling among the crowd. The streets are filled with restaurants, bars, stores, and various items being sold on makeshift carts. Matthias is delighted by what he sees, as are his friends. They decide to explore the first bar they come across. They are immediately intrigued by the number of ladies socializing with the men. Matthias and his friends are captivated.

Matthias and his friends find the area to be a playground, but they need immediate cash to be able to do the things they want. They manage to secure a job delivering supplies from the warehouse to the fruit market and make a few dollars. The men thoroughly enjoy the city's nightlife and make sure to visit every bar they can find in order to flirt with the ladies. Matthias, being the most handsome of the six, attracts most of the ladies while his friends stay close by his side.

A week passes, and all the passengers show up as instructed. Matthias notices that Captain Blitz's clipper is still docked at the harbor. Half of his crew deserted the voyage, and numerous attempts are made to find them. Captain Blitz doesn't have enough crew members to continue the journey and must recruit more men. Efforts are being made to hire additional seamen, but the news of the disastrous voyage makes the men uneasy about sailing with Captain Blitz.

Matthias and the passengers listen to the leaders who speak Portuguese and are responsible for giving instructions to the crowd. Once again, lines are formed according to skills. The workers are divided based on their skills: masons, blacksmiths, farmers, dairy workers, metal workers, and craftsmen. They are assigned to different working groups and transported by horse carriage to various locations throughout the San Francisco Bay area for their work. Matthias, Michael, Dennis, Frank, Miguel, and Jose are all farmers and are assigned to the same workgroup, allowing them to stay together as they had promised. Alongside other men, they are taken to a farm in San Jose, a considerable distance away, to start working immediately.

Matthias and his friends' initial job is to cultivate the land for the spring crops, which include potatoes, broccoli, asparagus, artichokes, and lettuce. The land is challenging to work with, and much of the work is done by hand. Matthias and his friends use shovels and hoes to till the land. Sometimes, oxen, donkeys, or horses are employed to assist with soil tilling and irrigation. The six men find themselves engaged in the same work they did in their cherished homeland. Their aspiration for a better life was to acquire a new skill in their new country, far from the arduous toil of farming, which was familiar to them. However, instead, the men are assigned to a farm that is in great demand and is a highly desired trade among immigrants. Engaging in farming will allow them to remain united, a commitment they made to each other before embarking on their journey.

Chapter Eleven

Matthias, Frank, Michael, Dennis, Miguel, and Jose are taken to a small two-room cottage to share. They are thrilled to be living together. They check out the place. There is a gathering area with a wood-burning stove in the corner of the room and a wooden table with four chairs. There is a separate bedroom that serves all six men. There are only two single beds in the bedroom so the men take turns for the most comfortable sleeping arrangements: two of the six young men sleep on the beds, while the other four sleep on the floor on blankets. They alternate the sharing of the beds every third night. There is no running water in the cottage. There is a privy behind the building for the community to share. The water well is located in the center of the courtyard and provides water to the emigrant community.

The cottage is located at the end of a long building that is used by the supervisors and foremen. There are several other cottages used by emigrants who settled in from previous voyages and are already working the fields when Matthias and his five friends arrive. The men are cramped in the tiny cottage, but it is more spacious than their arrangements on the Clipper ship. They settle down to their new quarters and learn to share everything they earn and barter for the things they need. They become shrewd businessmen.

Portugal had one of the highest rates of immigration from Europe by the middle of the twentieth century with most Portuguêse emigrants to the United States. Around 1870, the majority of early Portuguêse immigrants were men from the Azores, a group of islands and islets in the North Atlantic Ocean. Matthias and his friends are a few immigrants that came from Madeira and settled in the San Francisco Bay Area. Most Madeirans settled in Hawaii or the Eastern part of the United States, especially in the New England states, because of the fishing trade. Matthias and his friends adapt nicely to their new living conditions and their new homeland.

The men begin working in fields and feel very comfortable working alongside other Portuguêse emigrants and others from Mexico, England, and Spain. Because of the language barrier, the six men feel more comfortable together in their common language. They adapt nicely with other emigrants who also keep to their ethnic group so they too can communicate with their kind. Most of all they all manage to communicate by using sign language and facial expressions. Each ethnic group seeks others from their native country and lives close to each other for security and the ability to communicate and bond as a community.

Working in the fields is hard work and it is true that the work goes from sunup to sundown. It brings back memories of the hard work Matthias did alongside his father and brothers. Yet, he feels a sense of freedom. The Idea of being with friends his age, sharing the place together, and earning money of his own makes him work even harder. Having a place to live and work is enough to give him a sense of freedom.

Matthias is a hard worker and devoted to his bosses. He becomes totally immersed in his work with the goal of eventually bettering himself. He, along with his friends, does not have to think about school; besides, they do not have time to take off to attend. Living among the Portuguêse community provides him with everything he needs and lacks the incentive to go to school or learn English; it never enters his mind the importance of learning the language.

Matthias remains content in his Portuguêse community and begins to develop a lot of friends who speak Portuguêse. He does have a good mind for dealings in business - a skill his father taught him as a young man. He has a delightful personality and charming mannerisms, which enhances his ability to work well with people. This serves him well in his new life in America.

His charm and good looks attract a lot of young ladies. Matthias is by far the most distinguished-looking of his five young friends and stands above them in height. His friends tease him about his loose flirtation with the ladies who are drawn to him. After the hard work through the week, they go wild on weekends. Mathias loves the wine that often gets him into trouble. Every weekend, the friends go to parties that begin on Friday night and end late into Sunday night. The freedom they experience in the new world is a reflection of what they all dreamed of; money to spend, no parents directing their every move, parties, wine, and ladies galore. "What a life," Matthias says.

Chapter Twelve

The San Francisco Bay area begins to prosper at the turn of the twentieth century with the influx of workers. Many more Europeans follow Matthias and his friends to America for the opportunity to work and a chance for a better life. There are a lot of folks who have previously caravanned to California during the gold rush and never left. San Francisco and the surrounding towns surged in population. Many ethnic groups stick together for comfort and to understand each other including the Portuguêse. The strong economy in San Francisco is bursting with activities and the development of housing and businesses everywhere. This was before the disastrous earthquake.

In April 1906, the San Francisco earthquake struck the coast of Northern California at 5:12 a.m. on Wednesday, April 18, with an estimated magnitude of 7.9 and a maximum Mercalli intensity of XI (Extreme). High-intensity shaking was felt from Eureka on the north coast to the Salinas Valley, an agricultural region to the south of the San Francisco Bay area. A devastating fire soon broke out in the city and lasted for several days. Thousands of homes were destroyed. A range of 700 to 3,000+ people died and over 80% of the city of San Francisco was destroyed. The events will be remembered as one of the worst and deadliest earthquakes in the history of the United States. Matthias and his friends wake to the earth shaking under their feet and don't know what to think. They had never experienced such a terrifying incident in their life. They are terrified, and so are the other workers in the camp. Everyone comes outside the housing and are all staring at each other wondering what has happened. The San Jose area where they are staying is spared major losses.

As people run outside their homes he witnesses a panic scene. He has a flash back of passengers panicking on the clipper ship. As he tries to walk over to comfort women and children the earth suddenly shakes under his feet again and he falls to the ground. People manage to seek each other for comfort. The ground stabilizes, but everyone questions, what happened? The foreman in charge explains that San Francisco had a terrible earthquake.

The earthquake in San Francisco and surrounding areas is devastating and inflicts considerable damage on several cities. San Francisco downtown is essentially destroyed. As damaging as the earthquake is, so are the aftershocks. The fires break out and burn out of control, creating more destruction. Approximately 80% of the total destruction was the result of the subsequent fires; within three days, over 30 fires erupted caused by ruptured gas mains. Many folks are evacuated from San Francisco to nearby cities. Nearby cities pitched in to help where they can in the relief effort.

The communities where Matthias and his friends live likewise pitch in to help. Their cottages are open to strangers or anyone who needed a place to live temporarily. Although very crowded, the community gathered their resources to assist those in need. Housing was provided along with food and even temporary jobs when needed for many folks. The farms were eager for extra helping hands.

As months pass, the folks start their life over. People whose homes are totally destroyed managed to resettle in surrounding cities like San Jose, Santa Clara, Sunnyvale, Los Gatos and others where they start a new life. Others go back home to scavenge what little remains of their home to rebuild.

Almost immediately after the quake (and even during the disaster), planning and reconstruction plans were hatched to quickly rebuild the city. Rebuilding funds were immediately tied up by the fact that virtually all the major banks had been sites of the conflagration, requiring a lengthy wait of seven to ten days before their fire-proof vaults could cool sufficiently to be safely opened. The Bank of Italy (now Bank of America) had evacuated its funds and was able to provide liquidity in the immediate aftermath. Its president also immediately chartered and financed the sending of two ships to return with shiploads of lumber from Washington and Oregon mills, which provided the initial reconstruction materials and surge of rebuilding started.

The Army built 5,610 redwood and fir "relief houses" to accommodate 20,000 displaced people. The houses were designed by Mathias McLaren, and were grouped in eleven camps, packed close to each other and rented to people for two dollars per month until rebuilding was completed. They were painted navy blue, partly to blend in with the site and partly because the military had large quantities of navy blue paint on hand. The camps had a peak population of 16,448 people, but by 1907, most people had moved out. The camps were then re-used as garages, storage spaces, or shops. The cottages cost, on average, $100 to build. The $2 monthly rent went towards the full purchase price of $50.

Chapter Thirteen

In July 1906 the wild parties get old and the men decide to settle down. They get tired of spending money on booze and women. Michael, Miguel, Frank, Dennis, and Jose have been courting young ladies for a while and decide to commit to marriage.

It is not so for Jose and Matthias. They make plans to continue to live together to share expenses. They no longer pursue the wild parties and women.

Jose is the same age as Matthias. They develop a close relationship more than the other four friends. They rely on each other more as they bond and become like brothers. Jose speaks English and writes which provides a necessity for Mathias.

Michael is the first to marry; on July 6, 1908, he married a young lady named Rita from the Azores. They settle down in a small house in Santa Clara and raise a family of three girls. Michael works in a co-op on a Santa Clara farm with other Portuguêse and eventually buys his own land and starts to grow peach fruit trees.

In 1894 the Altrurian Cooperative Councils, based in Oakland, organized the first cooperative store system in the urban Bay Area. In 1899 representatives of a number of co-op stores in rural California communities came together in Oakland and organized the Pacific Coast Cooperative Union (PCCU). The Portuguêse community formed their own co-op to help families who need assistance to start a new life in America.

Rita is a wonderful wife and mother and devotes her time to raising their three daughters. They have a very successful business and become well intertwined into the fabric of the Portuguêse social life.

Frank married on October 15, 1908, to a young lady named Louise who arrived from Lisbon Portugal. After their marriage, Frank starts working in a dairy in Los Gatos and earns enough respect due to his hard work to become in charge of the daily operations. He gains enough knowledge to start a dairy of his own. He goes into a partnership with another co-worker named Mark and both men are able to obtain a loan from the co-op to purchase enough land to start their own dairy. They buy ten cows and a bull as a starter. The business flourished and both men became prosperous. At one point they build the herd to 100 cows.

Louise is not a farm girl and doesn't like working on the dairy. She stays home and is consistently homesick and miserable. Frank senses how miserable Louise is and how she will never adjust to this type of living. It saddens him to see her this way. Louise finds herself very lonely staying home.

Frank and Mark work well together and are very generous with their business. They provide a lot of job opportunities for new emigrant arrivals who lack the basic skills to earn a living. The emigrants are offered jobs at the dairy which becomes a recruiting opportunity for Frank and Mark. Eventually, the new hires earn enough money to go on their own.

As time goes by Louise continues to be very unhappy at the dairy. They do not have children after six years of trying. Frank decides to sell his portion of the business to Mark. Frank contemplates sailing to (Hawaii his original destination) to prevent him from returning to Madeira. He shares his thoughts with Louise. She is thrilled that Frank is willing to move for a possible better life away from the dairy. Ok! Frank says. "Let's prepare to embark to Hawaii on the next available ship." Louise is thrilled!

Six months later the six men meet at the San Francisco Harbor to bid the happy couple a farewell. This trip will be in luxury by traveling on a steamship. Frank feels more confident on this voyage compared to his clipper ship ordeal. The men watches Frank and Louise board the huge steamship. The remaining five men are awe-struck at the massive ship. They stand at the dock until the ship fades into the vast sea as the bright sun camouflages their sight as the steamer glides off and disappears into the horizon. The sendoff creates a melancholy feeling among the men so they decide to go to the nearest pub to have a few drinks as they always did to lift their spirits.

A steamship, often referred to as a steamer, is a type of steam-powered vessel, typically ocean-faring and seaworthy, that is propelled by one or more steam engines that typically move (turn) propellers or paddlewheels.

The age of steam did not, of course, replace the age of sail immediately and there was a brief period when sailing ships, including the clippers, were fitted with auxiliary steam power. The traditional wool clippers were still plying the Australia run in the 1890s. But inevitably, they were the last of their breed.

On December 12, 1908, Miguel is the next to marry. He selects a young lady named Jane who recently arrived from the Azores, Portugal. She too does not know anything about farm life. Miguel decides not to farm. He joins a co-op with three other families to invest in a vineyard. Co-ops are very popular and essential because it affords families an opportunity to pull their resources together to help those who want to buy land or start a business. Jane agrees and settles down to work alongside her husband at the vineyard. They have three boys, Anthony, Carlos, and Alexander, who learn the ins and outs of working and managing the vineyard. His sons remain loyal to their parents and stay and learn the family business. Eventually, Anthony, Carlos, and Alexander buy out their parents and take over the business when their father becomes too frail to work.

On April 4, 1910, Dennis married Margarita who recently arrived with her parents, a well-to-do family from Madeira. With all good intentions, Margarita tries to adjust to her new married life and her husband's business but like Jane, she never adjusts to living away from the life she once knew in Madeira. Margarita is extremely homesick and desperate to return home. She craves being back into her social life in Madeira. Her parents missed the prestige that their wealth provides in Madeira and they cannot find this status in America. They returned to the island as soon as Margarita got married. Margarita is a bit spoiled by the high standard of living her father provided for her and wants to return with them. It was her aunt's idea that she join her parent in America.

Dennis debates what he should do to make his wife happy. He was not all thrilled with his life in America so he asked Margarita if she would like to return to the Island. She is thrilled with the idea of departing and cannot wait to do so. He has saved up a lot of money and both decide to take their money and return to Madeira to start their own tailoring business. Again, the four men with wives join Dennis and Margarita at the San Francisco Harbor to bid them farewell. They will travel in a steamship, a luxury from their old clipper days. They fade away as the evening sun sets on the horizon never to see them again.

Jose and Matthias become shrewd businessmen and both have saved a substantial sum of money. Every chance they get they turn their hard-earned cash into gold bullion. Frank manages to save enough gold bullion to purchase a tract of land in the foothills of the east side of San Jose and starts an apricot orchard. He later relates to Matthias the difficult hard work it took to get the crop started and to keep it going. Had he known, he says; "The work involved I would have reconsidered planting another crop."

Apricots are a fragile fruit that requires being picked by hand and put into buckets. Workers get paid by the number of buckets they pick at the end of each day. The apricots are processed right on the ranch.

The buckets are dumped into large flat crates. An assembly line of workers cut the fruit in half gently removing the pit and laying them facing up on large flat wooden trays. They are placed neatly in a row and taken to a smudge house. A sulfur can is ignited and the door shut, this process will treat the fruit prior to drying. The next day the apricots are set out to dry under the hot sun for about two weeks. They are packaged into bags and taken to the market. After a few years of hard work, Jose builds a successful business.

Jose feels he is now ready to marry and start a family. On June 10, 1911, he married Dolores. She is well-established in the Bay area with her family. The family owns and manages a huge fruit distribution business in Santa Clara. Jose and Dolores have been courting for a few years and get along like best friends. The wedding is a huge celebration where guests from all over the Bay Area are invited. The celebration goes on for three days where the wine and food flow freely along with several bands playing the guests' favorite tunes.

Jose and Dolores desire to have a family but they have no children. She devotes her energies to helping her husband with his business.

Chapter Fourteen

September 12, 1914, is a very hot day and Jose is eager for lunch. It is past lunch hour and Jose keeps looking for Dolores who brings their lunch every day. He waits and is surprised that she has not arrived. He is puzzled not to see her after several hours without lunch he is exhausted and thirsty and decides to go home.

Jose enters the modest home they built together and nicely decorated in Dolores' favorite colors of bold blues and browns. He notices a vase filled with fresh Black Eye Susan's in the middle of the coffee table. He looks around and calls out her name but gets no response. He walks around the house and at last to the kitchen where he expects to see her. He sees only his lunch half-packed sitting on the kitchen table but no Dolores. Again, he pauses and calls out her name. He starts walking to the window to see if she is out back picking vegetables. All he sees are a couple of monarch butterflies leaping from one flower to the next.

Jose is puzzled not able to locate her. It is not like Dolores to neglect lunch they look forward to each day. Then he hears a muffled noise coming from the back porch. Of course he says, she must be doing laundry and forgot about lunch. He rushes out to see and it was only the breeze kicking the screen door. He looks out the door and finds Dolores sprawled out on the porch faced down with half of her body hanging over the wooden deck leading to the garden.

Jose is horrified. He leaps to the ground grabs Dolores and turns her over and pleads for her to wake up. He starts to gently shake her and rubs her face and chest. He begins to scream with eyes filled with tears. "Help! Help somebody! Help!" Finally, reality sets in that she is dead. He does not want to accept it and continues to scream for help. He cries and sways back and forth as he holds her close to his heart and will not let her go. He is lost in his sorrow as he continues to embrace her and rocks her back and forth sobbing.

A workman, Phillip, comes by and hears the screaming and crying, and witnesses the scene. Phillip realizes he must do something to help his boss. He puts his arms around Jose who has become his best friend and gently pulls the lifeless body of Dolores away from Jose. Phillip takes Dolores into the house while Jose remains kneeling on the ground trying to grasp what just happened. Later the doctor says, "Your wife died of a stroke, Jose."

Jose never gets over the devastation of losing the love of his life and refuses to remarry. He seeks the comfort of his remaining friends; Matthias, and Miguel, but the void is never filled by the loss of his wife. They remain friends and live close to each other over the years. He works on his property until he can no longer work

Mathias decided he had had enough of courting and entertaining women. He decides to seriously look for a wife. He is already well known among the Portuguêse community who consider him a great catch. In spring, the Holy Spirit Festival at Five Wounds Catholic Church in East Side San Jose is where it all began. There he strikes up a conversation with a lovely young lady he has not seen previously at the festivals. She introduces herself as Mary. She is sixteen years his junior and recently arrived from Madeira Island. Matthias finds her to be very beautiful and young which appeals to Matthias. Mary is one of the very few Madeiran girls he has met in years. Most Madeirans do not settle in California. They prefer Hawaii for farming or the New England states for fishing opportunities. This provides a common core for conversation and they learn they have many things in common. Mary is taken by his handsome look, charm, and his humor. Its love at first sight for both.

Chapter Fifteen

The first decade of the 20th century saw increasing diplomatic tension between the European great powers. This reached a breaking point on June 28, 1914, when a Bosnian Serb named Gavrilo Princip assassinated Archduke Franz Ferdinand, heir to the Austro-Hungarian throne. Austria-Hungary held Serbia responsible and declared war on July twenty-eight. Russia came to Serbia's defense, and by August 4, Germany, France, and Britain were drawn in as well as America.

World War I was one of the deadliest wars in history and resulted in an estimated nine million soldiers' deaths and twenty-three million wounded, while five million civilians died due to military action, hunger, and disease. Millions more died as a result of genocide, and the devastation of the war heavily contributed to the 1918 Spanish flu pandemic.

During the First World War, most women were barred from voting or serving in military combat roles. Many saw the war as an opportunity to not only serve their countries but to gain more rights and independence. With millions of men away from home, women filled manufacturing and agricultural positions on the home front. Others provided support on the front lines as nurses, doctors, ambulance drivers, translators, and, in rare cases, on the battlefield.

The war does not affect Matthias or his friends because the government needs farmers. There are a lot of non-farmers who are drafted into the war and many volunteer. It affects many families and women start taking over jobs the men left behind.

On October 12, 1915, Matthias and Mary married in the Five Wounds Catholic Church on East Side San Jose. The church is packed with family and friends. After the ceremony, a procession starts around the nearby neighborhood where neighbors have prepared food and drinks for the couple as they march from one home to another. The wedding celebration lasts about three days. There is a lot of singing, dancing, and drinking as it is the custom among the Portuguêse when couples get married or any special occasion that lends to a celebration.

Matthias and Mary settle down in a tiny home he bought from Frank after he moved out a few years ago. The home is modest with three bedrooms, one bath, a kitchen, and a small living room enough to start a new life with Mary and raise a family. She refurbishes the home to her desire and taste and makes the home an attractive cozy place.

The house is located on Fourth Street in downtown San Jose close to his work and not too far from Five Wounds Catholic Church where he met Mary. They worship every Sunday and during the week where they spend a lot of time participating in church family activities. The convenience of the horse-drawn carriage on First Street directly takes them to the church. The church community becomes their home away from home. It provides a retreat to fill the loneliness of family back in Madeira. They mingle with the community and gain lots of friends.

Matthias becomes too busy and finds himself being left behind by his church friends and the community. He still has no time to learn the English language and does not read or write in Portuguêse. In many ways, he is a stubborn man who focuses only on hard work and parties whenever he can and finds no need for schooling. Matthias makes time to drive around with his friends and sometimes he drives their car but never gets a driver's license. This complicates things when Mary wants to go places. Matthias learns to rely on his friends and public transportation for his needs. Mary likewise does not speak English and she tends to follow her husband's way of life. Like many of his friends, they all drive around town without licenses and never get stopped by the police. It is not yet a law.

Chapter Sixteen

There were three major waves of Portuguêse immigration to the San Francisco bay area. The first wave was from 1850 to 1880, predominantly for the Gold Rush and whaling. Matthias and his friends arrive in the second major Portuguêse immigration wave, from 1880 to 1923 for economic opportunity.

The next wave was from 1960 to the 1970s, following the Capelinhos volcano's eruption on the Island of Faial, Azores Portuguêse in 1957. Senator Kennedy, along with fellow Members of Congress, passed the Faial Relief Act allowing 1,500 people from Faial Island Azores to emigrate most coming to the Bay Area. The population of Faial Island declined from 30,000 before the Capelinhos Volcano eruption, to 15,000 in the next few months. The San Francisco Bay area took one in ten of these Azores Islanders fleeing the volcano's death and destruction.

In California, there was a greater effort to maintain ethnicity. The Portuguêse emigrates generally settled in rural areas where they farmed or operated dairies and fruit orchards. They hired other Portuguêse as hands to help them with their business, and under these semi-isolated conditions, it was easier to preserve their old customs. Fathers were the decision-makers of the household. They allowed their daughters to attend school only as long as the law required. After that, they kept them at home. Boys enjoyed more freedom than girls, but they also attended school and were required to work every single available moment for their parents. The whole family was expected to work on the farm or dairy. When the rate of emigrates slowed and American-born descendants far outnumbered the foreign-born Portuguêse, assimilation began.

As emigrants arrive they settle in and start to build their community or move into one already established. People from the same country; English, Mexicans, Germans, Italians, and others bought or build homes next to each other. They started small businesses to provide food and buy homemade goods, meats, home grown fruits, and vegetables or barter for things they did not have. They erected clothing stores, shoe repair shops, tailor shops, radio stations, television programs, and many others to the demand of the growing communities.

Portuguêse Americans have assimilated quietly into the fabric of American society. They tend not to use politics as a means of promoting their own welfare. They also tend to avoid political and social protest. They are self-reliant and avail themselves of welfare programs only as a last resort. They have organized themselves through mutual aid societies as well as civic, educational, social, and fraternal organizations. Some of these include the Portuguêse Union of businesses. The emigrants establish a self-sufficient cultural community to provide for their daily needs and make a profit. Matthias and his friends still feel very comfortable that everything they need is available to them and have no need to pursue an education or learn the language. This is typical of the first generation of emigrates when they reach the new world. This makes Matthias and his friends feel right at home. The community festivals provided a lot of the homeland traditions brought over from the homeland and a place for everyone to meet. The festivals are well established by the time Matthias and his friends arrive.

Chapter Seventeen

At each festival, Matthias looks forward to the popular Portuguêse food called malasadas, which are deep-fried pastries, similar to the *beignet* of New Orleans that traditionally have no holes or fillings but are coated in granulated sugar. These pastries are an important cultural food in Madeira and the Azores. You can still find Malasadas throughout the San Francisco Bay area throughout the Portuguêse festivals.

A popular Portuguêse tradition in the Bay Area is the Holy Ghost Festival, which is celebrated each May with a parade and festival. This three-day event is not an official church holiday, but a traditional observance that began in the 18th century in the Azores. The Holy Ghost festival goes back to when Queen Isabel, wife of Portugal's King Dom Diniz, 1296, won a battle in Alvalade. Fresh from the victory, she vowed to remember the blessing of the Holy Ghost each year by holding an annual festival in which the poor would be fed free of charge.

The festival queen is the human embodiment of this spirit of generosity. Her procession leads the crowd to the Portuguêse Hall where meat, cabbage, and French bread donated by Portuguêse ranchers, are cooked earlier by volunteers. Cooks use huge stainless steel kettles to prepare the beef and broth with spices and cabbage. French bread is sliced and put into large bowls. The broth with meat is poured on top of the sliced French bread and a sprig of mint is added as a garnish on top. A long line of servers serves the large steel bowls on the center of each table, family style. The servers monitor the bowls to make sure they are immediately refilled until everyone is fed.

The meal is free to the public for anyone who wishes to partake. Hundreds of people participate in this free meal that is served in several sittings to accommodate everyone. Later as years pass the meal becomes well known and many who are not Portuguêse show up for a meal. As the tradition continues to gain in popularity tickets are issued in advance to make sure there is enough food. Walk-ins hang around for leftovers and often times they get fed.

Matthias always looks forward to having a Linguica (leeng-QUEE-sah) sausage sandwich at every Portuguêse festival. It reminds him of his grandmother preparing the chorizo and blood sausage and hanging it from the ceiling over the blazing embers in the tiny kitchen. The aroma of the sausage creates a burning desire to have one. Grandmother pulled the sausage down as needed to flavor the meals or to eat sliced-in homemade bread. The Linguica sausage is similar to chorizo but made with different spices and cuts of pork. At the festivals, it is cut into hot dog bun size, grilled, and served in a soft crust French bun covered with mustard.

The Portuguêse mingle at the festivals. They share words of new arrivals, and daily success stories from the old homeland, and simply enjoy each other. It is at these festivals where they share hardships and identify needs in their community. When there is a need the community huddles together to assist a struggling family or individual to get back on their feet.

In 1915 Matthias travels by horse and carriage like most folks do to pick up friends along the way. The car revolution is in its infancy and many folks cannot afford to buy one the closest Portuguêse Association for the festivals is in East Side San Jose. It has taken many years to build the church and required many hours of dedicated volunteer work which Matthias assisted and is very proud to admire the church every time he visits.

Chapter Eighteen

By 1920 cars were readily available and Matthias could travel to other cities like; Santa Clara, Hayward, Milpitas, and Los Gatos to name a few, and to attend more festivals during the summer weekends with friends. Each city puts on its own festival each year and it is common for folks to travel from one festival to another throughout northern and central California. It is something every family looks forward to and plans to attend. Often time's friends squeeze into a car for the joy of riding and for the fellowship and meeting friends along the way.

Through the years the festivals became bigger as each city tried to outdo the other. Musicians come from Portugal to perform. Big celebrities like Amalia Rodrigues who is known as the queen of FADO and who made it famous would later come to the bay area from Portugal on her American tour.

The Fado is a very melancholy type of song unique to Portugal. It is performed in central Portugal bars of Lisbon late into the night and in the early hours of the morning. These songs are believed to have originated among Portuguêse sailors who had to spend months or even years at sea away from their family's beloved homeland.

The Portuguêse love the Fado, meaning "fate," that praises the beauties of the country for which the singer is homesick or for the love one left behind. Many entertainers come from Portugal and perform wonderful music at the festivals through the years. Folklore dancing groups assemble locally and come from afar to enlighten the emigrants as they sing, dance, and participate in the festivities. If they do not know how to dance or sing someone is eager to teach them. It is this community that that cradles Matthias as he learns the Azorean customs which differ slightly from his Madeiran upbringing.

Chapter Nineteen

In the early 1900s, the government did not have provisions to assist retirees once they were too old to work. As the years went by men became too weak to work and start to retire. The government came up with a plan: men who worked in the fields for twenty years or more were given land acreage based on the number of years they worked.

The federal government issued 160-acre tracts virtually free to about 400,000 families who settled new land under the Homestead Act of 1862. Even larger numbers purchased lands at very low interest from the federal government. The first years of the 20th century were prosperous for all American farmers and emigrants.

Matthias continues to work as a contract laborer for the Government. His family begins to grow with his first child a daughter, named Frances. The second is a boy named Manuel and there would be another three girls; Rosie, Virginia, and Jane all born in the 1920s.

By early 1930 Matthias decides to go out on his own. He worked for over thirty years for the government. He receives many acres of land on the east side of San Jose in a place called Alum Rock Hills. Other emigrants who work a few years for the government are given the opportunity to buy land at a very reasonable price and many do to start their own businesses including Frank who is already settled into his own property.

He moved his family from downtown San Jose to the east side of San Jose where his land is located. The property comes with an old farm house much bigger than their current dwelling. It contains four bedrooms with plenty of room for the kids. Mary and the girls decorate the inside of the home with wallpaper and paint. The children are excited about the additional room the house offers

Matthias turns his large acreage into a fruit orchard and small patch to farm and provide for the family's needs. He plants peaches and produces enough money to support his family of seven. He barters and sells the remaining to the local markets and friends. His orchard grows peaches, along with various types of herbs in a large garden.

Matthias loves animals and his farm is filled with chickens, ducks, pigs, goats, two horses, two donkeys, and a cow that helps him cultivate the land. Work is very difficult, using oxen, donkeys, and horses to do most of the hard labor in the fields. It requires many hired hands to trim the peach trees, fertilize, and assist with harvest. The farm comes alive when word gets out that it is harvest time. Workers show up in droves to work the harvest. Matthias depends on hired help to harvest the fruit and works alongside the workers until the harvest it complete.

The bulk of Matthias' day is spent in the field. He eats breakfast and starts his early day at sunrise. After feeding the stock (horse, cow, goats, chickens, and pigs), common chores take the form of plowing, hauling, and pruning. Watering, and harvesting. It is a life filled with hard physical labor but Matthias loves it. Still, he can attend church, lodge meetings, dances, picnics, visits with friends, and family gatherings. He enjoys everything about his orchard, farm, and the community he calls home.

Everyone in the family has to work long hours. The daughters and sons dread the harvest season because they work two to three hours before leaving for school and another three to four hours after they arrive home. His wife Mary works double time keeping the house running, feeding the animals, and preparing meals for the family often times even for the workers who assist Mathias.

The daily routine during harvest is very demanding when workers: Mexican, Portuguêse, and others who want a quick buck arrive early in the morning. They are given each a bucket and a ladder when needed and sent to the field. The peaches are picked and poured into wooden crates and loaded on horse-drawn wagons. As time goes by with the use of trucks the farmers including Matthias are able to speed up the process of getting the large harvest to San Jose and Santa Clara markets. A foreman keeps track of the number of buckets the fruit pickers fill. At the end of each day, Matthias pays the workers for the number of filled buckets. They return the following morning and continue to work until the harvest is complete, usually, one to two weeks depending on the number of workers. When the harvest is done the workers move on to the next ranch or farm and continue to work until the harvest season is over.

A few years later, on a freezing afternoon, Matthias returns home from working in the field. It is a cold day in May 14, 1943. He finds his wife Mary of many years sprawled lifeless on the couch in their living room. The children, who are not home at the time, except for his son Manual who is working in the field all became suspicious of Dad. He drinks a lot and gets a bit deviant when he is drunk. The children suspect foul play but nothing is confirmed. The actual cause of death is declared as a heart attack.

Dying young is not uncommon for women because of raising many children and working the difficult demands of farming. Mary takes on too many duties out of necessity. She and her son are always in the field when Matthias needs assistance, especially during harvest. Mary leaves in the morning while the kettles cook lunch unattended providing a hot meal for the workers. She and her son became a life line for Matthias on the demands of working the land.

The long marriage had many difficulties with Matthias' drinking and demands. There are a lot of arguments but they managed to stay together in desperation of needing each other to survive. Matthias is devastated at the loss of his wife. Shortly after her funeral he begins to lose interest in his orchard and farm and neglects many of the required chores to keep it running. His drinking increases with each day. He finds himself alone with Manual who is constantly exhausted after work. Mary's death pushes Matthias over the edge.

Finding himself alone with Manual overwhelmed him and ponders what to do next. Now in his early seventies, he lacks the energy required to perform the daunting daily tasks on his land alone with Manuel. He cannot afford to hire permanent workers required to help him with the work needed. He finally realizes just how important Mary was in his life - she was a work horse. At times his friends pitch in to help him and cheer him up but they have their responsibilities and it is only temporary. The daunting realization kicks in and he starts thinking of selling the property and is pressured by a market salesman to sell.

Matthias' son Manual helps his Dad as much as he can but again, the work required becomes too much for him. He decides to join the Army right away and tells his Dad he was drafted and had no choice so his Dad will not try to keep him from leaving. He anticipates coming home to help his father with his business when the war is over.

World War II was a global conflict that lasted from 1939 to 1945. The vast majority of the world's countries, including all the great powers, fought as part of two opposing military alliances: the Allies and the Axis. Many participating countries invested all available economic, industrial, and scientific capabilities into this total war, blurring the distinction between civilian and military resources. Manual sees a great opportunity to get way from his Dad for a while he sees the war as a means to escape.

There is a huge outcry for men and women to join the military serve. In late 1943 Manual joins the Army and after basic training, he is immediately assigned to the 509th Infantry Battalion and is shipped to Europe. Eight months later he is wounded by a grenade assault under heavy fighting.

Chapter Twenty

Matthias hangs on to the land until his son returns home. Manual is wounded in battle that left his left leg crushed and had to be amputated which causes him to be discharged from the Army after nine months.

In 1944 he returned home. Matthias is dumbfounded when he sees his son walking towards him dragging his left leg. The prosthesis installed in place of his left leg prevents him from bending his knee. He walks very slowly and with a stiff left leg. This injury prevents Manual from performing efficiently on the orchard and farm and leaves his father speechless. Matthias is devastated to see his son handicapped and unable to walk properly.

Manual gets a job working for social services as a foster parent for two grown extremely mentally ill men who often have violent rages and pick fights with Manual. His training in the Army helps him deal with the men's aggression. The temperament isolates Manual from contacting and visiting family and friends. The men are unpredictable and cannot be trusted around people. They cannot be left alone in fear of what they may do.

Manual becomes the men's father. A neighbor who usually sees Manual roaming around the yard does not see him today and calls the police. Police arrive and find the fifty-eight-year-old lying dead on the living room floor. The two men, Waldo and Larry, are sitting on the couch staring expressionless into thin air. The manual has been dead for about three days but the men did not have the sense to call for help.

The police cannot gather any information on what happened because Waldo and Larry are mentally incapable of speaking. Their form of speech is only a loud grunt. There are bruises and a few cuts around Manuel's face and neck which puzzles the policemen. Matthias and the family are suspecting the men killed Manuel on one of their violent rages. The cause of death was never determined.

Matthias cannot depend on his daughters: Frances, Jeannie, Rose, and Jane to do heavy work around the house when they can. They try but like most young women their age they have other things they rather do. They do what they can to keep their father at bay and leave in peace. They join the Portuguêse community society where they spend a lot of time against their father's wishes. The girls all try to figure out how they can escape living with their father. He becomes more demanding after Mary dies. A Portuguêse custom is for girls not to leave home unless they get married. The girls devise a plan to marry as soon as they can to live.

Frances being the eldest of five girls gets married at age seventeen to escape the grueling daily duties required by her stern father. Her marriage to a young Englishman is not approved by her father so she elopes to Lake Tahoe and leaves on a sour note. Frances has one son named John but he becomes estranged and never goes to see his grandfather. Through the years Frances seldom returns to visit her father. When she does, it is always by herself. Matthias, who could not control Frances when she was young, has no control over her now and cannot demand for her to come and visit more often. She works at White Front Department Store located in El Camino Real and fades away into the American fabric of social life. Frances dies at eighty-five years old of natural causes.

Most Portuguêse children do not have a childhood due to the isolated distance from their friends to play with. Their childhood is spent at the Portuguêse church and social hall in the late evenings or weekends. All they know is hard labor so they do whatever they can to escape the daily burdens that are levied on them. This creates resentment between the children and their parents. None of Mathias children went beyond a high school education because of the powerful demand for long hours of hard work on the property

Matthias' daughters learned to speak Portuguêse as young children at home as did all first generation of emigrant children. They learn their Portuguêse heritage at home but as most grew up they have no interest in staying at the ranch or farm with their parents. They fade away from their family culture to be intertwined into the city life that they so eagerly seek. The children attend American schools because the law requires it but the need to work the land is much greater to include Matthias, out of desperation he makes his daughters work every moment he can.

Jeannie marries a young Italian named Larry who has no interest in working on the farm. They have no children. She remains a housewife for a few years and eventually divorces. She takes a job as a waitress at Original Joe's Italian Restaurant on First Street in downtown San Jose until she retires. She succumbed to a severe stroke that left her paralyzed and speechless. She dies at age fifty-three in a nursing home in Santa Clara. Rosie goes wild, parties with her fiancé, and enjoys the military life has to offer. The Non-Commission Officers Club at the Navy Station supplies them with many activities away from the farm. She gets tattoos on her arms because that is the vogue of the day with other military wives. She relishes every moment with excitement at the new life she has chosen. Rosie and Frenchie marry when he leaves the Navy to work for a construction company located in Santa Clara. They buy a modest three-bedroom home where they settle to raise a family.

Rosie marries at age seventeen to a Frenchman named Frenchie who is stationed at Moffatt Field Navy Station located in the Bay area. She becomes a military wife. Moffett Field was commissioned in 1933 as a naval air station to support a "lighter-than-air" (LTA) program. The LTA program involved training pilots to fly blimps and servicing the aircraft.

They have four children, two girls and two boys. She stays home as a housewife to raise her children and sees them off on their own. They adopted a baby girl named Dee Dee to raise. The story goes that Rosie's younger daughter, Sally, got pregnant in high school, and Frenchie and Rosie take the baby in. They raise Dee Dee through college. She attended Santa Barbara California University and got a job in Washington State and seldom comes home to visit. Rosie dies at age fifty-seven from a long battle with bone cancer devastating Frenchie at the loss of his beloved wife.

Jane, the youngest, makes Matthias happy when she marries a Portuguêse man named Frank. But Frank, like the others, prefers working as a truck driver rather than farming. They have a son, named Frank Jr. Jane stays home most of the time and works at a seasonal job for Dole Cannery in San Jose and rises to Floor Supervisor. The cannery hires mostly women and Jane plays a large role in hiring a lot of Portuguêse women. She hires Amalia at age seventeen to work the midnight shift. They work hard canning apricots, peaches, pears, tomatoes, and prunes. The work requires long hours standing but the pay is great. The job includes evenings, midnight shifts, and weekends. She retires from Dole and dies of Melanoma at age fifty-eight. Her husband Frank died ten years earlier at age forty-nine from alcoholism.

Devastated and alone, Matthias realizes he can no longer manage the huge workload by himself. He breaks down in tears and considers himself a failure. He thinks of the old times and his wild dreams of pursuing a better life. He suddenly becomes homesick for the family in Madeira, and he decides to sell the property to an investment firm that has been pressuring him to sell for some time. The company wants to turn his land into a golf course. In 1946 he sold the land. He settles the deal in cash with gold bullion and buys a triplex apartment on Sherwood Avenue. The layout for each is one bedroom, a living room, a kitchen, and a bathroom home located near Santa Clara Catholic University. It is close to a bus stop that takes him to the Portuguêse hall and church. His property is located on the Santa Clara and San Jose county lines. Most importantly it is very close to his friend Jose who lives down the street.

Sherwood Drive

The two apartments are located in the front of the building and one in the rear. It has a two-car detached garage and a small yard he can plow into a garden. He selects one of the front apartments for himself and rents the other two for income. He has money saved and buried under his house. He creates a crawl space in the living room closet where he can descend under the house to where he has buried his cash whenever he needs money.

The 1929 depression left many people not trusting banks and they lost their life savings. This generation becomes jaded to saving institutions and clings to their money by stashing it in mattresses and other hidden places in their home. Without a retirement income, Matthias must secure his savings to last a long time and rely heavily on the rent to supplement what he has saved.

Shortly after he moves into his new home he starts to rent the two apartments to two Portuguêse families who just arrived in America. They are faithful in paying the rent each month. He does not have to worry about not speaking English since he speaks their language. As time goes by he rents to Americans and asks his friend Jose who lives at the end of Sherwood Drive to interpret for him. He gets along well with his tenants and learns to accept them as family. He shares his vegetables and fruit from his garden during harvest with them. He is very proud of the quality of his garden. The acquired skill from the orchard he grafts a plum tree to bear four different types of plums and has a huge peach tree with peaches the size of grapefruits. The largest peaches you will ever find.

Chapter Twenty-One

Matthias became rather bored and restless living in the city with nothing to keep him busy. I guess you can say he went from feast to famine. He does not have hobbies and he does not care about sports. All he knows is to work and manage his garden. One day he decides to start making burgundy wine, (probably not a good idea since drinking is already a problem for him). Matthias gets with Dennis who is a successful wine maker in Napa Valley. He spends a few days at his vineyard to learn the ins and outs of wine-making to perfect his skills. He is extremely interested in going into the business of making wine and makes every effort to learn all he can until he feels comfortable to go home and start his new adventure.

He invests some money to make sure he has everything he needs. He still does not drive and has to rely on his friends to get the supplies he needs. He turns his two-car garage into a wine-making room and wine storage. He purchases ten large wooden barrels already seasoned to hold the wine and places them on cement blocks in two rows on one side of his detached garage. The room will remain dark during the wine storage.

He buys a huge grape vat big enough to hold a ton of concord grapes with room for several barefooted people to stomp the grapes. He buys the wine press that is proudly displayed at the entrance to the garage. He is ready to go. He contacts Dennis in Napa Valley and orders a ton of grapes to start the process of wine-making. He is good at planning everything to the finest detail. The project fills his time but it is an involved process that requires a lot of help. To assist him get started he invites his family and friends to the house for an all-day party and grape stomping. They are intrigued by Matthias' new adventure and are eager to see how it all works.

The concord grapes arrive by truck and he immediately contacts his family and friends. Everyone shows up including grandkids. Each crate of grapes is taken from the truck bed and dumped into the vat. Five ladies and a couple of kids all plunge into the vat and start stomping grapes. There is a lot of chatter and laughter as they form a circle at times dancing around inside the vat until the grapes are crushed. The ladies and kids climb out of the vat with purple-colored feet, legs, and thighs. They hose down to get clean but the purple stains cling on for a few days. The grapes are left in the vat for a couple of weeks to ferment. After two weeks the men take over, they use shovels to scoop the fermented grapes into the waiting wine press.

Fighting the bees and flies the grapes are pressed until every ounce of juice is collected into buckets and poured into the barrels until filled. Matthias adds the necessary amount of sugar, then lights a sulfur stick and puts one in each barrel before he hammers the top with a wooden cork to seal the barrels. The wine will remain in the barrels to age in a dark room to be used as needed. Sometimes the wine stays in the barrels for years prior to being tapped. Every five years or so, as demand necessitates, Matthias repeats the process and again family and friends show up to stomp grapes and have a huge party of eating, drinking, and dancing. This is his highlight of the year. He is in his element watching his family and friends have a wonderful time. He is no exception; Matthias has always been the life of the party from his younger days. After a day of celebration, everyone takes a couple of full wine jugs home with refills freely given whenever they want. Matthias donates most of the wine to family, friends, and neighbors and to the Portuguêse festivals in Santa Clara. He never sells his fine wine, though his friends encourage him to do so for extra money.

Chapter Twenty-Two

In May 1948, Mathias began to dream of going back to the homestead to see his family. He is now seventy-six years old. He contacts a Portuguêse travel agent, Mr. Nunes, who has an office located in the Portuguêse hall in Santa Clara and makes all the arrangements for the trip. He is amazed to be traveling by airplane from California to Chicago to New York to Lisbon, Portugal, and by ship. It takes him a couple of days to reach his destination. He actually enjoys the trip. He cannot help reliving the horrible old voyage on the clipper ship.

He arrives in Funchal harbor, the Capital city of Madeira. As he steps off the small boat carrying passengers to the dock, he stops and gazes with amazement at the development taking place. The city is bursting with tourists, and people walking to and fro. Cars are seen driving all around Funchal competing for street space with the ox-drawn carriages that were once the means of transportation in the city. It reminds him of San Francisco harbor when he arrived in America. He manages to walk around until he finds a boarding home for his stay.

During the nineteenth and twentieth centuries, Madeira became one of the first tourist destinations in Europe mostly visited by European aristocracy of the time. The good air of the island and its landscapes were recommended by doctors to patients undermined by tuberculosis. Many came here to convalesce, as did writer Julio Dinis and later Winston Churchill for his love of painting. Matthias is exposed to a bursting economy that he has not witnessed before in Madeira.

The following day he arranges to go and visit Santo the Serra located up in the high mountains. The boarding housekeeper, Susana, informs him that he can now take a bus to Santo da Serra. "It makes a run once a day," she says. "Great!" Matthias says. He walks a short distance to the bus station located at the seaside to catch the bus.

He is eager to ride up the mountain to see his family and the homestead he once lived. He wants to share his life adventures with them. When he arrives at the Santo da Serra homestead, he finds out that his immediate family has all passed away. None of his brothers or any of his immediate family he knew at age eighteen is alive. Matthias is devastated with a broken heart for not being able to see his family. On the old homestead where he once ran up the mountains with ease to work alongside his father and brothers, he can no longer climb. He sits on top of a hill overlooking the steep valley below, puts his hands over his face, and breaks into tears as he longs so much for what he has lost.

While visiting his old homestead he does find a childhood friend named Manual de Aveiro who still lives three houses away from his old home and develops a close relationship. He was able to remember Mathias' family and related a lot of details of how his family often talked about him and wondered about Mathias' life and whether he was successful. Manual, his friend, has six children, four girls and two boys. His second to the eldest is a girl by the name of Conceicao. She is known to be a bit of a wild young lady and takes an interest in Mathias. Mathias being the handsome and flirty gentleman plays along. Matthias is still handsome for his age. Conceicao already has a little boy out of wedlock named Jose, a disgrace to the family, and the church community. She loves to drink and enjoys men's companionship.

Her father takes care of her little boy named Jose. She flirts with Matthias and is asked to stay with Manual but he decides to stay with his niece on his inherited property. He stays a few days to visit and mingle with everyone. They have one celebration after another to cheer for his arrival, everyone on the mountainside is invited. Matthias loves everything about the community he once knew. This place is a time capsule. It stands still as nothing has changed since he left. There is still no electricity or running water in the homes. The privy is located a few yards away but everyone seems happy, "Incredible!" as he reflects on his past. Matthias gets updates from remaining kin and old family friends as they fill the gap of his absence. He finds out he has nine nieces, several nephews, and cousins he did not know he had. His parents left him some property near Manual's home but his nieces live in his parents' home and take care of the land. Matthias is okay with that arrangement and lets them continue to manage the property.

Conceicao runs around flirting not only with Matthias but others in the local area. She becomes pregnant without her parent's knowledge. She tries to hide her tummy by wearing loose clothing but eventually, the hidden secret is revealed. Having any child out of wedlock is highly frowned upon by the family and the Catholic community, having two, she is banned from the family.

With her secret discovered, Conceicao is labeled and treated like a harlot by her father and the community including the church. Humiliated by her actions her father kicks her out of his home. She decides to move to the city of Funchal to find a job to support herself while Jose, her firstborn, who is one and a half years old stays with her parents. She finds out that working as a housekeeper cannot support her. In her late pregnancy, she returns back to Santo da Serra where Matthias is still living near her parents. She sees Matthias a lot and they become friends.

The baby was born on May 10, 1949, and she is named Amalia. The city of Machico located down the mountain by the seaside has a law that any baby born at home must be registered before thirty days of birth. Amalia's family totally forgot about the law and arrived to register the baby on June 11th, they were asked, "When was the baby born?" they looked at each other and said, "This morning." So Amalia's birthday is June 11th.

Shortly thereafter Manuel asks Matthias if he would be Amalia's godfather at her upcoming baptism. He agrees. Matthias made a commitment to take care of Amalia because Conceicao would not reveal the father's name. In those days, a Godfather took over the father's responsibilities for the child's care.

Matthias was in Madeira for over a year, and his daughter Virginia living in San Jose, California goes to the immigration office to extend his visa so he can stay over a year in Madeira.

A big celebration is being held to celebrate St Anthony's Day. It is being held near his boarding house and he is invited to attend along with friends he meets in Funchal. Matthias flaunts his charm and gives the impression he is wealthy. He dresses sharp with his gold watch sparkling and manicured hair. It is at this celebration he meets Mami. He is immediately smitten with her beautiful, petite figure and charm. He starts calling her a doll and clings to her every moment he can. Mami's mother notices his obsessive and infatuation he has for her daughter and devises what she thinks is a perfect plan to get her daughter to America. She approaches Mami who is twenty-two years old and engaged to be married to Roberto.

Mami's mother encourages her to marry the old goat so he can take her to America. Her mother insists that he is already in his seventies and probably won't live much longer. Her mother arranges a meeting with the couple to encourage Mami and her fiancé to delay their marriage until Matthias passes away. The couple hesitantly agrees. The mother goes on to say that Matthias is rich and you will benefit from his wealth. You can marry Roberto and you both can go back to America.

Chapter Twenty-Three

Mami is not as sweet as she appears. She has a personality that can change at a minute's notice with an uncontrollable temper. Matthias is too blind and enchanted and does not notice the spontaneous meltdown she has with her mother.

She is a bit spoiled being the youngest child of four girls. Her father provided well for the family. She had her own personal maid to care for her. She was the apple of her Dad's eye until he divorced the family and left for the Continent leaving his family destitute.

Mami is small-framed woman, barely four feet, four inches tall, and 100 pounds. She handles herself with poise and dresses in well-tailored clothes, a reflection of her upbringing. She displays deep black hollow eyes with a pale complexion and black hair. She commands attention when she speaks with her boisterous high-pitched voice. Matthias is enthralled with everything sees in her. He is determined to ask for her hand in marriage.

In October 1949, he marries the twenty-two-year-old Mami. His new wife rushes around to obtain a passport and prepare for their departure to America. They stay in a hotel in Funchal a few nights prior to departure. Conceicao visits them in the Hotel and offers baby Amalia to Matthias and Mami. "Here take Amalia. She is your baby take her." Devastated, Mami looks at Matthias dumbfounded and asks him, "What does this mean?" Mami thinks the woman just wanted to give up her baby to a married couple but immediately says, "No, I do not want a new baby, people will think I had the baby before marriage." She looks puzzled as the mother and child walk away.

Conceicao approaches the couple several times while they are still in the hotel and begs them to take Amalia with them. But young Mami insists she does not want an infant. Conceicao is not able to provide care for Amalia and places her in an orphanage in Funchal where she will remain until she is five and a half years old.

When her grandfather finds out that Amalia is going to be moved to another orphanage, he goes and checks her out and takes her to his homestead up in the mountains where she will remain until almost eleven years old.

Chapter Twenty-Four

A few years later Matthias is troubled and remembers his promise to Manuel that he would take care of Amalia. He talks with Mami who adamantly refuses to bring Amalia to America. She says, "Why not bring my niece who is about Amalia's age?" Mathias says, "No! I promised Manual I would take care of her."

He contacts a Portuguêse lawyer to start proceedings to bring Amalia to live with him and his wife Mami in San Jose, California. Mami rebels against his promise. She says, "Absolutely No!" Instead, Matthias is firm in his decision and he does not relent on his promise. Mami continues her stern objection through the immigration process. She will not give up the fight. She continues to harass him through the legal process that takes several years to finalize. Mami tries desperately to convince him at the very last minute not to bring Amalia. This is a battle she will not win.

Matthias learns that Amalia must arrive in America prior to May 30, 1960. The law that allows a child with only one parent to be adopted will end at the end of the month. Amalia must enter New York prior to that date or she will be denied entry.

On 1 May 10, 1960, after a long wait, Matthias and Mami travel to Madeira Island to vacation and to pick up Amalia who is now almost eleven years old living with her grandfather, Manual. Matthias is thrilled to finally be able to fulfill his promise to Manual. There is a great welcome celebration given by Manual in honor of Matthias' arrival and to honor their loyal friendship. The surrounding community participates in the celebration. There is wine flowing freely, men huddling around a pit cooking beef on a skewer, fresh homemade bread, and various musical instruments. Folks bring what they have to complement the celebration. They play familiar folklore music and they sing and dance. The party goes on all day and into the night. Matthias is in his element. He loves parties and has a great time. Conceicao does not attend the festivities. She lives in Funchal and things have not been well with her parents since she put Amalia in the orphanage.

Mami meets Amalia at this celebration. Amalia is scared to death as she glances at her new potential parents. Mami immediately dislikes Amalia as she sees her niece standing beside her. Mami's mother approaches her insisting, "Taking Amalia is a bad choice." Mami envies Amalia and explains to her mother the situation and her frustration with Matthias' determination to bring Amalia instead of her niece. After the celebration, the couple returns to Funchal to their hotel while Amalia stays with her grandparents to pack.

On this trip, Mami asks her mother to arrange a secret meeting between her and Roberto, her waiting fiancé. When they meet each other, the dormant passion reignites as if time stood still. It has been almost eleven years since they departed after her wedding; Roberto is still waiting for her. They kiss and embrace for a long time but the thrill is short-lived. Roberto breaks the news that he can no longer wait for her, after all, he gently says, "It has been eleven years and I cannot wait. I want to marry and have a family." Mami is devastated and breaks down in tears. She begins to sob uncontrollably and becomes violently ill from the news. Her contract marriage to Matthias was never expected to last this long and now she is losing the love of her life. Roberto tries to calm her down and they embrace again for a long time.

He slowly lets her go and walks away looking back as she sobs. She watches him fade away as he turns the corner at the end of the street and disappears. As they depart her heart sinks with remorse and they never see each other again.

Prior to dinner, Amalia sits on her favorite spot, her eyes scanned the west side of the mountain, and she could see the dotting of sparse houses embedded along the mountainside; some with red tile roofs and others with thatched roofs. Her eyes follow the mountains steep valley below. At a distance, the rocky narrow Ribeira de Machico (river) intertwines with each turn and eventually fades away disappearing along the narrow valley as it enters the town of Machico and blends in with the sea. Her attention is drawn to a cruise liner gliding at a distance. It appeared like a miniature ship gliding along the vast ocean. She ponders, "Where is that ship going?" Amalia tries to focus on every detail her eyes can see, only to barely notice the dots that are windows on the side of the ship a soft trail of smoke as it exits the center smoke stack and fades into the air. The ship gently vanishes beyond the cliffs that drape down into the sea.

Her eyes followed the ship and picked up the mountain cliffs on the east side of the valley. She could see the terrace fields as they sloped gently down the mountains which had been prepared for early spring planting. She noticed the rich patchwork of reddish-brown turned soil and narrow water channels installed to carry water from the main lavadas (irrigation channels) down the side of the mountain. As her eyes flow upward to the mountain top, she sees a lush, green grass carpet covering the mountainsides and the laurel trees that stand high on the mountain top. She continues to follow the mountain until she makes a full circle. What a beautiful sight of emerald greens and patchwork of terrace farms. Amalia can feel the dew and the clouds creeping in over the mountain which will eventually camouflage the beautiful scene. It was times like these she relished living at her grandparent's homestead. Now she is prepping herself to meet her new potential parents, the people who will take her to America.

The night prior to meeting her new parents at the dock Amalia's family has a wonderful dinner celebration for Amalia's farewell. Her grandparents, aunts, uncles, and cousins all huddle in the little kitchen and enjoy a fest. There is a lot of talk about the wonderful things Amalia is going to have when she reaches America and how she will be so well taken care of. Her grandfather, tells Amalia to accept her new family and to be good to them.

Chapter Twenty-Five

Amalia does not have her own bedroom in her new home. She is thrilled to sleep in the long narrow hallway next to the floor heater. Strict house rules require she to go to bed promptly at eight P.M. every night including weekends. Matthias and Mami who go to bed much later have to step over Amalia while she sleeps. In the evenings she takes her cot out of the hallway closet; unrolls it; and puts a sheet and blanket over top. In the morning she rolls the mattress and puts it back in the closet. Amalia does not mind the arrangement. It is better than the straw bed she shared with her Aunt Teresa in Madeira.

Amalia is enrolled in Hester Elementary School in San Jose. She is eleven years old when she is enrolled in third grade because she is too old to start in first grade as Mami insists. The principal says, "She is too told to start in first grade." Mami continues, "I insist!" but the principal says, "NO! We will start her in third grade and see how she does."

Matthias is extremely jealous of his beautiful wife and becomes obsessed over the years as he gets older and she continues to blossom and becomes more beautiful. Matthias drinks his homemade wine regularly and often gets drunk and becomes violent. When Mami married him she expected to be rich and live a rich lifestyle like her father provided for her and the family. Instead, when Mami arrives in America she finds a poor old man barely getting by on two hundred dollars a month rent from his apartments. She has to immediately find work to support both of them and now three. Not speaking any

English and with no occupational training, she has a dilemma on what to do. She secures a job at Mott's Cannery processing fruit. It is a seasonal job but provides adequate money to hold them over until the following year. They live three blocks away from Mott's Cannery so she is able to walk to work. There she starts to learn the English language but it will be minimal just enough to get by.

Matthias becomes more obsessed with the fact Mami is gone all day. He starts walking her to work meeting her for lunch and walking to meet her after work. Walking Mami to work is ok for a while but then Mami puts her foot down and says she no longer wants him to hang around her all the time. Problems get worse as Matthias loses control of Mami and takes his frustrations on more drinking. Mami starts flirting with the men she works with and develops a friendship with a young man her age. Home life for Mami is miserable and lashes out at Amalia when things do not go her way. Every time she looks at Amalia she relives the battle she had with Matthias not to bring her, Amalia becomes a thorn in her side, and Mami simply dislikes her and makes Amalia responsible for all her failures.

The trip to Madeira changed Mami. Perhaps, she did not overcome the loss of her fiancé. She would never be the same and Matthias notices it but attributes it to Amalia. She feels hopeless in a marriage she did not want and now she has Amalia to contend with.

Mami and Matthias begin to have more frequent fights. At one point he becomes so violent, that Matthias threatens to kill her. Mami is so frightened she calls the police who have a difficult time controlling Matthias upon arrival. The two officers drag him outside and lay him face down on the lawn to handcuff him. The officer asks if Mami wants to press charges of domestic violence but she refuses.

All the commotion creates a spectacle in the neighborhood. Amalia hears the noise and runs home from her friend Emma's house across the street. She is horrified to see Matthias on the ground and the officers overshadowing his body. Amalia cries and becomes sick to her stomach at the scene.

Chapter Twenty-Six

Amalia notices how unhappy Mami is and how she often gets angry and vicious for no reason. She has frequent attitude changes and mood swings with an evil streak. She lashes out at Amalia and profusely beats her using whatever instruments she can grab: kitchen spoons, fireplace instruments, belts, but mostly her strong forceful hands.

Mami, outburst creates a very unpleasant situation for Amalia and especially Matthias who ignites her temper when he becomes violent when drunk. Matthias becomes more jealous of his beautiful wife as she becomes more independent and draws attention at every festival they attend. The men especially are drawn to her for her unique petite figure. The two when alone become like wild animals trying to outdo the other with loud screams, name-calling, and attacking each other's persona. Amalia is always in the middle trying to calm them both to no avail.

The outbursts become more violent and Amalia is terrified when they take place. Mami cries all the time in her unhappy life. Amalia wedges herself between Matthias and Mami when they draw knives at each other. In tears, Amalia begs them to stop as she struggles to push them apart. This is the environment Amalia finds herself with her new family.

A year, after they arrive in San Jose from Madeira Mami, is at her lowest point and tries to commit suicide. Amalia, a vivacious eleven-year-old is outside playing with wild feral cats roaming around the yard that she has adopted as pets. She decides to go inside the house for lunch. She finds Mami sprawled on the couch with a bottle of pills open and empty on the floor. Amalia unsuccessful tries to wake Mami to no avail. She tries again and again by shaking her and calling out her name. Amalia is terrified not knowing what to do. She still does not speak English and Matthias is nowhere to be seen.

Amalia calls Jane who speaks Portuguêse. She panics and frantically explains to Jane what is going on. Jane does not know if Amalia is telling the truth. Jane tries to calm her down by saying, "She's probably sleeping." Amalia says, "NO! NO! I tried to wake her several times and she is not responding. She convinces Jane to call for help. Jane asks, "Where is Dad?" "I do not know," she says. "He is not here," Amalia says. As Jane tries to calm Amalia she senses an urgency to call for an ambulance. "I will call for an ambulance," she says. "Amalia, let the emergency team into the house when they arrive," Jane says.

Jane says, "Stay on the phone until the emergency crew arrives." They arrive and Amalia hands them the phone for Jane to talk with them. Amalia crying goes searching for Mathias in the yard. She cannot locate him anywhere. (She later learns he was at his friend's Jose house.) He is beside himself when he finds out the news.

Amalia finds out that if the rescue team had arrived five minutes later at the hospital, it would have been too late to save Mami. For a long time, Mami will not forgive Amalia for saving her life. This incident will prevent her from securing jobs because she is considered a high-risk employee by insurance companies and employers.

The following year Matthias' rear duplex catches fire. The raging fire fills the front duplex hallway with smoke where Amalia sleeps stretched out on her cot. Matthias tries to wake her up unsuccessfully due to the smoke. He goes outside to seek help from the fireman who just arrived. They rush in to get her. Amalia, still asleep, wakes up shivering from the cold in the fireman's arms. The rear duplex is burnt to the ground and the family has no other place to go, they decide to move back into the smoke-stanched house when it is declared safe by the fireman. Matthias rebuilt the apartment and it is lovely, bright inside, and modern, but only has one bedroom. The newly built apartment overshadows the two dated ones in the front of the house.

The fights get more violent between Mami and Matthias. Mami still holds a grudge for Amalia. It does not help when Matthias shows her with the attention that Mami so craves. Amalia for no reason becomes Mami's scapegoat. Amalia is terrified of her and walks on pins and needles around her to prevent an outburst.

Chapter Twenty-Seven

When Amalia first met Mami in 1960 she was 32 years old and looked young for her age. She handles herself with poise and dresses herself in well-tailored clothes. She relishes the style of the 50s and proudly displays white silk gloves and a snake-skin purse that dangled from her arm. Mami is always smiling at people she likes but when Mami gets angry she is as strong as an ox. As years flow by Mami's weight becomes uncontrollable. She can go to 150 pounds and down again to 100 pounds when she is under stress.

Later in life, Mami confines in Amalia how devastated she was to marry someone she did not love. She and her fiancé truly loved each other. Mami confied to Amalia that she was still a virgin after ten years of marriage to Matthias.

Amalia is desperate to escape living with Mami and Matthias. She longed to be back to the homestead in Madeira. One day Amalia was watching Dennis the Menace on TV and in a scene where he runs away from home with a little sack over his shoulders. Amalia decides to replicate the scene to get away because she does not want to live with them any longer.

Amalia craves her family at the homestead in Madeira. She cries every night lonely and unwanted. Amalia does learn to adore Matthias because of the kind affection he bestows on her.

Running away from home was not a good idea. A neighbor caught Amalia and invited her into her home for cookies and milk, something she could not refuse. When it got dark the neighbor heard sirens and sent Amalia home. Mami had called the police to file a missing child report. They are all shocked when Amalia enters the house. Mami insists Amalia go to jail to teach her a lesson to never run away again. So there went Amalia to the San Jose Juvenile Correction Center in San Jose where she spent two weeks in solitary confinement to keep her away from the bad girls.

Despite Mami's attitude towards Amalia, Matthias adored her and taught her how to cook and play card games; they spent afternoons playing whist, backgammon, and cribbage. He also teaches Amalia how to cook his favorite Portuguêse food. He teaches her what he knows about money and the facts of life. They create a bond never to be broken.

Mathias wants to adopt Amalia. Mami relents so Matthias daughter Jane drives them down to the San Jose Court House to start the proceeding for adoption. Matthias' intention has always been to adopt Amalia and give her his name. This day is an exciting day for Matthias.

The judge hears the case as he intently studies Matthias. The Judge denies the adoption. Matthias is devastated. The judge says, "At age eighty-eight, you are too old to be responsible for a twelve-year-old child." The judge continues, "Your wife who is much younger will have legal guardianship of the child until she reaches eighteen years of age." Jane interprets what the Judge says. Matthias walks out of the court room sits on the steps to the court house and sobs. He feels great sadness for Amalia because of Mami's relationship with her. He looks up at Mami and makes her promise she will never send Amalia back to Madeira.

After this incident, Mami is shocked to be given guardianship of Amalia. She now feels she has a chain around her neck for the next six years. Mami does not hide her outrage when she leaves the courthouse, she walks away shouting with anger, "Amalia, you will pay as long as you live with me. You will pay for the misery you have caused me." So it was, Amalia went through hell for the next six years. (Learn more about Amalia's life, read the book titled "Amalia" by M. C. De Aveiro, published by Dorrance Publishing.

Chapter Twenty-Eight

Matthias is troubled by the way Mami treats Amalia but there is not much he can do. When he watches Mami beat Amalia he says, "Stop you are going to kill this child." Mami, says, "Good!" The troubles continue to escalate between Matthias and Mami. He drinks more and continues to be more jealous and obsessed with her. Not only is Mami petite and pretty she also sings at the Portuguêse Festivals where she becomes known among the community. After a few years, she stops singing but she now drives her English Ford and has some freedom. She goes places with or without Matthias and leaves him home often. Her excuse for the car is to take Amalia to school and drive to work.

Mami continues to work at Mott's Cannery and develops a friendship with Waldo a co-worker and begins to have an affair. She seeks other men to fill the void of her loneliness for losing her fiancé. This affair made her realize she is still a virgin after twelve years of marriage and decides to leave Matthias. Mami craves the attention Waldo gives her and they fall in love. She is beside herself when Waldo shows her the intimacy of love she never knew.

Matthias' loses the love of his life after thirteen years of marriage. She takes Amalia with her not because she wants to but because the court gave sole guardianship her for Amalia's care. She recalls the judge, saying she could send Amalia back home if she did not want to take care of her or give her up for adoption. She promised Matthias she would not send her back.

Mami continues to see Waldo and he falls madly in love with her. He does not adjust well to his new life in America and longs to be back with his family in Madeira. He proposes to Mami and tells her he wants them to return to the Island. The fact she is not divorced and has Amalia she has no desire to return to Madeira. She says no. The relationship abruptly ends when Waldo quits his job and departs for the Island.

After thirteen years of marriage, Mami takes Amalia and moves out into a hotel a few blocks from Matthias' home. Amalia is sad and begs Mami to allow her to visit Matthias. She reluctantly agrees. Every chance Amalia gets she runs to him, taking a bus when the distance is too far to walk. Matthias looks forward to Amalia's visits. Around the holidays Amalia goes to visit because she loves his train display. The train tracks go all around the tiny living room floor. He shares everything he knows about his trains with Amalia. Matthias tells jokes and shares many stories about the old homestead and his voyage from Madeira on the clipper ship. Many stories are shared while they play with the trains. Matthias is like a little boy playing with his favorite toy.

When Amalia visits she cooks his favorite Portuguêse dishes that he taught her. They joke when comparing the quality of the meals to his. Seeing Amalia gives Mathias great joy and he shares with her.

Matthias used to say, "I want to live long enough to see you grow up and away from that demon that you live with." Later years, Jane says, "My Dad idolized you," which is something Amalia never realized when she grows up with him.

Amalia and Matthias

Matthias never regretted bringing Amalia to America. Of all of his children, she was a success story. Everything he hoped for his daughters, Amalia excelled. She started to work at a very young age to support Mami. Mami began to become ill with various diseases and could not hold a job. Amalia was caring, loyal, and dependable with much compassion for Mami, Matthias, and older people. She shared some of the passions Matthias cherished; they both loved nature, animals, and birds, cooking, and gardening. Amalia is very cheerful and outgoing like Mathias was in his younger days. She is a peacemaker when arguments break out and is always willing to help others. She visited him often with food, washed his clothes, cleaned his apartment, and visited. She was always appreciative of the sacrifice he made to bring her to America and the hell he went through with Mami because of her.

Chapter Twenty-Nine

One day while playing whist Amalia asks Mathias, "Hey, my mother was single, why did you not marry her?" He looks at her in surprise at the question and says, "I thought about it but your mother was sort wild with the men and I felt uncomfortable marrying her." Amalia responds, "I wonder who my father is?" Matthias looks with a smile at Amalia and responds, "I am the only father you will ever have." She stares at him for a moment and they continue on playing cards.

At age eighty-nine Matthias is diagnosed with leukemia and is given six months to live. Once he hears the news he refuses any kind of medical treatment. The doctors recommend against it but Matthias is a stubborn man and knows what he wants. He decides to live out his days at home and no longer makes doctor visits. Matthias lives another seven years with leukemia.

As time goes by with each of Amalia's visits she notices his health decline and becomes extremely weak. He confines in Amalia that he wants to live long enough to see her away from Mami and on her own.

In the meantime, Amalia is corresponding with a GI in Vietnam as a pen pal, a popular thing to do and highly encouraged for the morale of the troops. Through a friend she is given a mailing address for her to drop him a letter. She starts corresponding with a Staff sergeant named George. It is not long before he returns to the USA and visits his step-brother, Bob, who lives in Hayward. He contacts Amalia saying, "I am in the area and can we meet?" They make arrangements to meet at Matthias' house. One evening he shows up at her front door.

She opens the door and George is in awe when he sees Amalia. She is beautiful, slender, five feet four, with long medium brown hair, light brown hazel eyes, and very friendly. He is impressed with her. He returns to Langley Air Force Base in Virginia where he is stationed and immediately starts putting pressure on Amalia to marry him. "I do not know you very well. I have plans to finish high school and have a reporting date of July 20th to attend Transworld Airlines Steward School in Texas. I have a scholarship for LaRoy Beauty Academy, in San Jose. I am not ready to get married," she says.

George continues to pressure her. Life with Mami is a living hell. She thinks long and hard, she gives up her dreams and decides to marry him. She figures if he loves her she can learn to love him. He is so desperate to marry that he tries to get Amalia to marry him before she graduates from high school but this time she puts her foot down to a firm No! They set a wedding date in July.

July 5, 1969, Matthias is too weak to walk Amalia down the aisle to give her away but he is thrilled to see her get married and away from Mami. Amalia and her bridesmaids all dress at Mathias' home so he can see them all. Pictures are taken on his front lawn as he smiles with approval.

Thoughts run through his mind as he watches the priest perform the marriage ceremony. The young vivacious child playing cards and games with him, telling jokes, and laughing during her visits that he will dearly miss. Sadness overshadows the event when he knows he will not see her anymore after this day.

Amalia surprises Mathias the day after the wedding by coming for a last visit and to open the wedding gifts. Amalia intentionally arranged the visit to coincide with Mami being at work so she will not be there to see her leave. Amalia invites Jane who has become

Amalia's confident over the years. Jane gladly accepts the invite and shows up to see Amalia open the wedding presents and say goodbye.

Amalia starts opening the gifts while George cleans the Chevy Impala from the graffiti painted all over the car by the wedding party prank with shoe polish. After opening the gifts the couple stuffs everything into a U-Haul trailer. Says her good-byes and gets in the car. Jane has already left and Matthias walks out of the house and sits on his favorite chair glancing at Amalia as she gets in the car and waves. Amalia says to George, "Wait! Stop the car!" Amalia gets out of the car and runs to Mathias. She kneels down in front of him grabs his hands and cuddles them in hers. She looks straight into his tearful eyes and thanks him for everything he has done for her.

She invites Matthias to come with them to Virginia. With tears in his eyes, he says, "Newlyweds need time for themselves. Now that you are leaving, who will come to visit me and play cards?" She gives him a great big smile, kisses him, and hugs him as she departs. She gets back in the car and cries because deep down inside her heart she knows this is the last time she will see him alive. Mathias manages to wave while tears cascade down his chicks. He wipes them with that old handkerchief he always carries.

Matthias feels all alone once again. His children seldom come except for Jane who has been faithful with her visits over the years. He barely knows his six grandkids but does see them at Christmas.

Chapter Thirty

Now with Amalia gone life takes a different meaning for Matthias. He continues to stay in his home in San Jose but he no longer makes wine and his barrels stand empty except for one barrel that still provides enough wine to quench his thirst. The equipment remains idle in the garage full of cobwebs. His friends are all gone except for Jose and his family who barely come to his home to share wine with him. He drinks alone to hide the pain from the cancer that ravages his body.

Too weak to do anything around the house and yard, he looks over his overgrown garden filled with weeds and reminisces of the beautiful garden he once tended and enjoyed. His grafted plum tree that he once grafted still bears the four different types of plums. Matthias no longer desires the fruit. The tree reminds him of the vibrant days when he worked in his fruit orchard many years ago.

Matthias came to America under President William McKinley who served from 1897 to 1901 and was assassinated in office. He lived through thirteen presidents including President Richard Nixon who resigned from office. Mathias was intrigued by the thirteen presidents in his lifetime, he felt comfortable in the US government compared to the socialist government in Madeira. Matthias also lived and managed to escape five wars; Spanish American War, World War I, and II, the Korean War, and the Vietnam War.

All the friendships he developed over the years have faded away into the dust of life's end including three of his children. His loneliness makes him envious of his friends' passing. He cannot understand why he is still around.

In his final days, Matthias directs his attention to the feral cats that roam around the yard. He remembers how Amalia spent hours playing with them. They hunt mice in the vicinity of his home and gladly bring him peace offerings they catch and place them on the steps to the back door of the kitchen entrance. He loves his furry friends so much that he sits and watches them roam around the yard and come up to him to rub their furry bodies against his pant leg and occasionally play with them. They have now become his pets. Most of the cats come and go but there are a few who do stick around. They are special and help Matthias pass the days away. The furry friends become a daily entertainment. He cherishes them and looks forward to seeing them each morning as they eagerly await his presence proudly displaying a bowl with food.

On a sunny day, Jose pays Matthias a visit as he has many times before. Jose often takes Matthias for a ride in his proud antique Desoto that he has had for many years.

Jose notices that Matthias is much weaker now than he was at Amalia's wedding. He tries to make Matthias laugh and cheer him up like in the old days. Matthias is not in a jolly mood, now he is all alone he has no reason to be cheerful, his cancer pains are taking a toll.

They sit and reminisce about the old homestead on the island, their families and friends, and the wild women in their younger days. Jose says, "By the way, did they ever solve the case of the dead woman hanging on the tree up in the Alum Rock hills?" Matthias looks straight at Jose and says, "She was a very beautiful woman, and things just happen." Jose dies two weeks after their visit.

Matthias alone reflects on his life and feels he has completed his long life's journey; he is tired, loses his appetite, and has no will to live.

Matthias will never set eyes on Amalia again. He succumbs to the battle with cancer that he has quietly endured over the years. Alone and too weak to move he spends the days lying in bed. Mami who checks in on him, sees he is very weak and calls Amalia to come and see him. Amalia who is in Virginia lives from Payday to payday with George and does not have additional funds for a plane ticket.

Mami who lives in the back duplex does not see him walking around the yard or sitting on his favorite chair. She goes in to check on him and finds him peacefully lying on his bed. On September 1, 1969, Matthias fades away from this life to the ever after. After Matthias dies Mami buys a plane ticket for Amalia to attend the funeral. Amalia arrives at San Jose Airport on September 2nd to attend his funeral the next day. The funeral service is held at Saint Joseph Catholic Church in downtown San Jose where Amalia got married two months earlier. Amalia is saddened to lose Matthias' the only person she loved most in America.

Conclusion

This book deals with historical information relative to the Europeans and especially the Portuguêse people's lives and their escape for a better life. Matthias' journey like many others was a leap of faith that ignited a passion to pursue a dream to a foreign land with the possibility of a better life. The story is about this young man's journey to the unknown and the hurdles he overcomes along with his five friends. Matthias establishes himself and becomes successful through hard work and perseverance. However, Matthias' quest for a better life is detoured by many factors. He finds himself away from his family and doing the same work he ran away from in Madeira.

Matthias' story is like many others who ventured out on a leap of faith proving that sometimes dreams are not realized. Yet, many others do succeed beyond their wildest imagination. What Matthias ventures out to achieve is a single person's definition of success.

The journey is something Matthias never regretted taking but his losses were great. That leap of faith in a young man's journey reveals courage and determination are not to be taken for granted. Matthias has his *"rendezvous with destiny."* He endured losing his family and friends, no doubt his aspirations were of a grand scale to provide opportunities for himself and his family.

References/sources:

Matthias recounts his story with Amalia.

Wikipedia: Farm Life at the Turn of the Century:

Wikipedia, the free encyclopedia

Images of America - The Portuguese in San Jose, by Meg Rogers and the Portuguese Historical Museum

Google: History Farming and Madeira History

Pictures:

Wikipedia, historical photos; clipper ship

Private photos: Peach orchard, Sherwood Ave, and Amalia and Matthias

portuguesemuseum.org

About the Author

The Author was born in Madeira Island, Portugal, and immigrated to America as a young child. She later became a U.S. citizen. She achieved a distinguished forty-four year career in the private and public service. She is married and lives in Williamsburg, Virginia where she is currently involved in the local community. She continues write as one of her passions.

Made in the USA
Middletown, DE
24 June 2024

56192951R00068